The Blurred Blogger

TOM SWIFT

INVENTORS' ACADEMY

-BOOK 7-
The Blurred Blogger

VICTOR APPLETON

Aladdin
NEW YORK   LONDON   TORONTO   SYDNEY   NEW DELHI

ALADDIN

An imprint of Simon & Schuster Children's Publishing Division
1230 Avenue of the Americas, New York, New York 10020
First Aladdin hardcover edition June 2021
Text copyright © 2021 by Simon & Schuster, Inc.
Jacket illustration copyright © 2021 by Kevin Keele
TOM SWIFT, TOM SWIFT INVENTORS' ACADEMY, and related logos are trademarks of Simon & Schuster, Inc.
Also available in an Aladdin paperback edition.
All rights reserved, including the right of reproduction in whole or in part in any form.
ALADDIN and related logo are registered trademarks of Simon & Schuster, Inc.
For information about special discounts for bulk purchases, please contact Simon & Schuster Special Sales at 1-866-506-1949 or business@simonandschuster.com.
The Simon & Schuster Speakers Bureau can bring authors to your live event.
For more information or to book an event contact the Simon & Schuster Speakers Bureau at 1-866-248-3049 or visit our website at www.simonspeakers.com.
Jacket designed by Heather Palisi
Interior designed by Mike Rosamilia
The text of this book was set in Adobe Caslon Pro.
Manufactured in the United States of America 0521 FFG
10 9 8 7 6 5 4 3 2 1
Library of Congress Cataloging-in-Publication Data
Names: Appleton, Victor, author.
Title: The blurred blogger / Victor Appleton.
Description: New York : Aladdin, [2021] | Series: Tom Swift Inventors' Academy ; book 7 | Audience: Ages 8 to 12. | Summary: Tom and his friends track down a mysterious blogger who pushes pranks too far.
Identifiers: LCCN 2021000539 (print) | LCCN 2021000540 (eBook) | ISBN 9781534468924 (paperback) | ISBN 9781534468931 (hardcover) | ISBN 9781534468948 (eBook)
Subjects: CYAC: Inventors—Fiction. | Blogs—Fiction. | Practical jokes—Fiction. | Schools—Fiction. | Friendship—Fiction. | Science fiction.
Classification: LCC PZ7.A652 Bl 2021 (print) | LCC PZ7.A652 (eBook) | DDC [Fic]—dc23
LC record available at https://lccn.loc.gov/2021000539
LC eBook record available at https://lccn.loc.gov/2021000540

Contents

1

The Introduction Malfunction

"LOOK OUT!" I SHOUTED. "COMING THROUGH!"

I ducked around fellow students as I ran down the first-floor main corridor. Unfortunately, it was the beginning of the school day, so the hallway was buzzing with twelve- and thirteen-year-olds.

"Good thing we just charged him, huh?" Noah asked with an eye roll as he raced beside me.

Normally, my best friend Noah Newton was happy to join me in the pursuit of knowledge and scientific achievement. Now he joined me in the pursuit of our small robot, Raider. That's right. We were chasing our new robot all over our school.

That may sound weird, but believe it or not, it's not the first time something like this has happened here. It's not even the first time my friends and I have chased a robot through the halls. That's what happens when you attend a cool school like the Swift Academy of Science and Technology.

"Whoa!" Kent Jackson shouted as he sidestepped the speeding robot.

Our little robot's motor whined as he zigzagged past other student obstacles. His main housing was only half a meter square and fifteen centimeters tall. It looked kind of like an oversize, flat gift box. Noah and I had used the body of the battlebot we had made for Mrs. Scott's robotics class. That's right. We had a robot battle as a class project a while back! See? I told you it was a great school.

"Hey!" shouted Jessica Mercer as she jumped out of the way. "Aww ... that's cute!"

Noah and I had removed our battlebot's weapons and added a metallic dog head on top instead. He had cameras for eyes, and microphones hidden inside his pointed ears. It had been Noah's idea to make the snout triangular to look like his dog, Phoebe. The finished robot resembled a steampunk bull terrier piloting a flat car. He even had a tail—actually a Wi-Fi antenna—poking out the back.

"Excuse me! Sorry!" I said as I pushed past Terry Stephenson and his friends.

"New robot," I heard Noah call out behind me. "You know how it is."

Up ahead, Raider was making his way through the crowded hallway better than we were. The little guy dodged surprised students with ease as he zipped down the corridor. It looked like our robot's AI was as sharp as ever.

Raider's AI, or artificial intelligence, was part of the problem. Noah, who's a first-rate programmer, had designed a program that would learn and grow over time. The trouble was that he started the program very low on the evolutionary scale, at a level similar to a lizard brain's fight-or-flight instincts. Earlier, someone slammed a locker door, and since Raider can't fight, he chose flight.

"You sure you didn't add a stop command yet?" I asked over my shoulder as I sprinted in pursuit.

"You wanted to show Mrs. Scott where we were, remember?"

Okay, it's true. I was proud of what we'd accomplished so far. Even Raider's name was cool. His actual name was RAIDR, an acronym for: Roving Artificial Intelligent Dog Robot. Okay, it's not as elegant as SCUBA or TASER, but you get the idea. And yeah, "scuba" and "Taser" are real acronyms. Look them up!

I slowed my pace a bit as we neared the end of the corridor. Raider wouldn't let himself crash into the closed elevator door, so he was trapped. He would have to stop, and then one of us could simply flick the off switch on the back. Of course, the hall was a dead end until it wasn't. The elevator doors opened and a couple of students shuffled out. When Maggie Ortiz stepped inside, Raider zoomed in behind her.

I sped up again. "Hold the elevator!"

I don't know if it was that Maggie didn't hear me over the usual hallway noise or if she was just too surprised by Raider's sudden appearance—it might've been both—but I saw her back away just as the doors slid shut.

"Stairs!" Noah shouted.

"Stairs!" I agreed.

We veered to the right and began climbing the steps two at a time. Luckily, the elevator on this end of the school doesn't access the basement, so it could only go up. Unluckily, our progress slowed to a crawl as soon as we hit the landing. The stairwell seemed more congested than the hallway had been.

"You take the second floor," Noah suggested. "I'll cover the third."

"Good idea." I pushed my way as politely as possible toward the second-floor landing.

Above my head, I heard Noah's footfalls on the stairs, along with his own round of "Excuse me!" and "Sorry!"

I dashed onto the second floor and jetted for the elevator, but I was so focused on my destination that I didn't notice the backpack on the floor up ahead. I sure noticed it, though, when I tripped over it and hit the ground with a splat.

"Smooth move, Swift!" Jim Mills chuckled as he picked up his backpack. Then the larger kid bent down and hoisted me to my feet.

"Thanks," I said, rubbing my elbow.

So you might've noticed that I share a name with our

school. That's no coincidence. My father, Tom Swift Sr., founded the academy with the proceeds from his neighboring company, Swift Enterprises. I guess you could say that inventing and innovation run in the family. My dad's company is a major government contractor and comes up with all kinds of top secret stuff.

I never let the fact that my name is on the school go to my head, though. I try very hard to be a normal student like everyone else. Of course, it's kind of hard to blend in when you fall flat on your face in front of a corridor full of students as you're trying to catch a wayward robot.

I was so embarrassed after my spill, I barely registered the elevator doors sliding open. Before I knew it, Raider zipped out, leaving behind a stunned Maggie. I knelt as the robot raced right for me, breathing a sigh of relief as I reached out, ready to catch him. But then he took a hard right and sped down the second-floor hallway.

"Not again," I muttered, taking off after him.

There weren't as many students up here, so I knew I had a shot at catching up. What I hadn't counted on was Mr. Osborne rolling out a cart full of glass beakers and test tubes. The short, wiry man paused in the middle of the hallway and stared at the approaching robot. That was the absolute worst place to stop with a cart loaded with glassware. Raider showed no signs of slowing down. I felt a boulder form in my stomach.

Mr. Osborne's eyes widened as he threw both arms over the top of the cart, bracing for the impending crash.

But the impact never came.

Instead, Raider's pointed ears swiveled back and his head dropped into a triangular compartment in the main body. Even his Wi-Fi antenna tail lowered as he scooted underneath the cart, easily clearing the lower rack.

My feeling of dread morphed to pride.

"What the heck was that?" Mr. Osborne asked.

"I'll explain later," I said as I dashed around him.

The other teachers would've barely noticed a robot wandering around or a drone cruising through the school, but Mr. Osborne was new. He was filling in for Mrs. Gaines, teaching chemistry while she was on maternity leave.

Raider cleared the cart, and his head and tail returned to normal height as he careened down the hallway. I'd lost some ground dodging Mr. Osborne, so I poured on the speed, but unfortunately still had trouble gaining on our robot. I'll give it to Noah: He programmed that thing to dodge obstacles way too well. I felt clumsy as Raider easily jetted around legs, backpacks, and other obstacles. And it didn't help seeing several students whip out their phones to record the chase.

As Raider neared the elevator at the opposite end of the hallway, the doors opened. I groaned at the thought of running up another flight of stairs all over again. Worse yet, this time I wouldn't have anyone to head off Raider at one of the other levels.

A grin pulled at my lips when I realized who was standing inside the elevator—Amy Hsu, one of my very good friends.

"Amy!" I shouted. "Hold the doors!"

She glanced at the approaching robot and then back up at me. Assessing the situation perfectly, she stepped out of Raider's path as she reached for the elevator buttons. But as I skidded to a stop in front of the open elevator, something strange happened. A multicolored shower poured from the elevator ceiling. Amy squealed, suddenly covered in . . . confetti.

Laughter erupted around me, and I turned to see all

the students I'd run past now gathered in front of the elevator. Of course, most had their phones out, recording the incident.

Meanwhile, Amy, who usually never has so much as a wrinkle in her clothing or a hair out of place, was making a bird's nest of her head as she tried to shake out all the tiny pieces of confetti from her long black hair. The minuscule pieces of paper must've clogged Raider's cameras, since he kept bumping against the back of the elevator.

I took advantage of the moment, slogging through the piles of confetti, and flicked the power switch on Raider's back. He stopped moving.

"What happened?" Amy asked, still fighting with the colorful flecks.

I glanced up and spotted a large, flat plastic bin dangling from the elevator's ceiling. It was attached to a hinge and now slowly swung back and forth. A small latch on the ceiling would've attached to the loose end of the box, keeping it closed. A thin wire snaked away from the latch and down the wall, ending at a button positioned perfectly over the open elevator control. It had been placed so well, I probably wouldn't have noticed it if I hadn't been looking closely.

"What happened is you got pranked," I replied.

A curtain of hair covered Amy's face as she shook out more confetti. "Well, I don't like it."

Another burst of laughter made her pause, peeping out through the strands. She squeaked and her hands shot to her sides. Amy does not like being the center of attention.

Mr. Osborne poked his head into the elevator car and glanced around. "What's with this school?"

His comment was met with another round of laughter.

"Way to make a colorful entrance . . . Junior," said a familiar voice.

I cringed. I knew that voice all too well. There was only one person in the world who called me that. I turned to see Andrew Foger standing among the onlookers. His phone was out and recording, just like the others.

What was he doing here?

2

The Discounted
Encounter

LET ME BACK UP A BIT. I KNEW ANDREW FOGER
from way back when we were younger. My dad and his
dad had worked together. They were partners in my father's
first company. Of course, Andrew would tell you that my
dad actually worked *for* his dad. That was only true in the
sense that my father did all the work while Mr. Foger paid
for everything. But what did I know at the time? I was just
a little kid. A little kid who ended up getting into trouble a
lot because Andrew goaded me into testing all of the crazy
inventions we came up with.

Okay, maybe "goaded" is too strong a word. I've

11

always been an act-first-come-up-with-a-plan-later kind of a guy, even when I was a little kid. But, hey, when you fracture your wrist testing a homemade hang glider by jumping off the roof (thankfully only a one-story drop), you expect there to be consequences. What you don't expect is your friend to say the entire thing was your idea. And stuff like that happened a lot.

"Are you okay, Amy?" I asked as I dusted some confetti from her shoulder.

"I'm fine," she muttered. "Just really embarrassed." She brushed past me, making her way through the crowd of onlookers.

I bent down and grabbed Raider, turning the robot on his side, letting a mound of confetti pour to the elevator floor.

"Looks like someone got you good," Andrew said as he ran a hand through his frizzy blond hair. It looked the same as it had when we were kids, like Andrew didn't know what a comb was.

"What are you doing here?" I demanded.

"What's he doing here?" echoed Noah as he pushed through the crowd.

Noah had the *pleasure* of meeting Andrew a while

back when several of the academy students spent the weekend at a nearby summer camp. It had been a cool retreat meant to let us work on bigger outdoor inventions for a couple of days. Two other STEM schools participated, and we all competed against one another. Andrew was enrolled in one of our rival schools.

"I just transferred here from Bradley," Andrew replied, clapping a hand on my shoulder. "I'm a Swift Academy student now."

Noah and I exchanged a look. It was turning out to be a great day.

Principal Davenport pushed through the crowd and peered into the elevator. "What in the world. . . ." He brought his radio up and keyed the mic. "Mr. Jacobs? We need a cleanup in the east elevator, please. Second floor."

"Animal, vegetable, or mineral?" asked Mr. Jacobs's voice from the small radio. I guess that was his way of asking if anyone had hurled.

Mr. Davenport sighed. "Confetti."

"On my way," the custodian replied.

Mr. Osborne was still examining the contraption attached to the elevator ceiling. "Does this type of thing happen often here?"

"Sometimes," replied Mr. Davenport wearily. He removed his glasses and rubbed the bridge of his nose. "You get this many intelligent kids together in one place, and you have to keep on your toes." He turned to face the onlookers. "Speaking of . . . shouldn't you all be heading for class?"

And like that, the assembled students lowered their phones and dispersed.

I tried to join them, but Mr. Davenport caught my eye. "Ah, Mr. Swift. I see Mr. Foger found you. He tells me that you used to be close friends."

Andrew nodded. "That's right, sir."

"Good," replied Mr. Davenport. "Because I've mirrored his class schedule with yours."

I did my best to force a smile. "Great."

This day was getting better and better.

Noah reached for the robot in my arms and gave a sly grin. "I'll take Raider to robotics while you show your *friend* around."

I clutched Raider tighter for a second before finally handing him over. "Thanks," I replied through gritted teeth.

"I'd love to see your robotics lab," Andrew chimed in.

I nodded, flashing Noah a triumphant look. "Great, we'll all go."

With the elevator locked open and out of commission, we took the stairs up to the third floor. Since Noah had tried to ditch me with Andrew, I didn't feel so bad about him having to carry the heavy robot up the steps.

"Why Raider?" Andrew asked.

"It stands for Roving Artificial Intelligence Dog Robot," I explained.

"Artificial intelligence, huh?" Andrew asked with an eye roll. "Okay."

Noah couldn't help but rise to the challenge. "Raider has a cool program we designed, so he actually learns as he goes."

"So you taught it to run away from you?" Andrew asked. "That's all I saw it do. You didn't add any voice commands? That's one of the first things I did when I built my own robotic dog."

Noah sighed and shook his head. "I just have to adjust the sensitivity of his fight-or-flight response," he explained. "And we're adding voice commands with the next update."

I raised an eyebrow. "We are?"

"That's next on the list," he replied quickly, cutting an eye in Andrew's direction.

"You should've seen how he ducked under Mr. Osborne's cart, though," I said, before telling them how Raider's head and tail had retracted.

"Cool," he said as we reached the robotics lab.

The classroom had several large worktables spaced evenly. A number of first-period students were sitting on stools around the tables littered with robot arms, gears, and pulleys, while others filed in.

Noah set our robot against the wall next to one of the many large toolboxes.

"Huh," Andrew said, glancing over his shoulder back into the classroom as we left for the next stop on our tour. "I was hoping it would be bigger. Bradley's robotics lab is huge."

I opened my mouth to reply, but Noah beat me to it. "I guess the school decided to save a little space here since we can always go next door to Swift Enterprises and use their lab if we need to."

Andrew didn't have anything to say after that.

The three of us had just enough time to get to our lockers before heading to first period. Honestly, I was kind of dreading going to algebra with Andrew in tow. And it wasn't because Andrew was, well . . . Andrew. It was because Samantha Watson would be there. Like Amy and Noah, Sam's a really good friend, and the final member of the Formidable Foursome, as my dad likes to call us.

Back when we were all at that summer camp retreat, Andrew was behind all the Swift Academy inventions being sabotaged. Worse than that, he'd capitalized on a rumor that Sam was the saboteur. Unfortunately, I was the source of the rumor. I'd only been joking, and Sam had long since forgiven me, but I'm pretty sure she never forgave Andrew. I wasn't looking forward to her reaction when he suddenly joined us in class. Sam was a great person and all, but she has a devious side that is . . . well, honestly a little spooky.

Noah, Andrew, and I walked into the algebra class-room just as the bell rang. Noah and I quickly took our usual seats next to each other—Noah in front of Amy and me in front of Sam. I glanced back to see Andrew nervously slide into an empty desk in the back.

"All right, sports fans," Mr. Jenkins said, his stan-dard greeting to his students. "It seems we have a new student." He glanced down at a sheet of paper. "Andrew Foger, is it?"

"Yes, sir," Andrew replied.

I turned with the rest of the class as Andrew gave a nervous wave.

Mr. Jenkins dropped the paper onto his desk. "I'd have everyone introduce themselves, but we have a lot to cover today."

"I already know some students, sir," Andrew replied. "Besides, Tom and I go way back."

I hardly noticed what Andrew had said. I was too busy staring at the back of Sam's head. I could only imagine the expression of shock, horror, and/or disgust that I knew had to be on the other side of her short brown hair.

"Welcome to Swift Academy," someone said. To my surprise, it was Sam.

I stayed in position, focused on Andrew, while Sam and everyone else spun back around to face the front.

I raised an eyebrow and leaned in closer to her. "'Welcome to Swift Academy?'" I whispered.

Sam adjusted her glasses and shrugged, yet she had a gleam in her eye that I couldn't quite interpret.

Like I said—spooky.

3

The Indifferent Inspection

FOR THE REST OF MY MORNING CLASSES—I MEAN
our morning classes—Andrew went through the same
routine each time he was introduced to the class, making sure everyone knew that he and I were friends from
way back. After the third time, I couldn't sink into my
desk low enough.

I mean, I get how being the new kid in school can
be intimidating. I guess pointing out that you already
have a friend makes someone look less like an outsider. I just wished there was someone else he could
latch onto. Instead, thanks to Mr. Davenport, Andrew

would be in every one of my classes, every day.

At least I wouldn't be stuck with him for the entire year. Another cool thing about the academy is how they rotate classes. Need a break from history? How about a block of physics? Need a break from physics? You can ramp it up to astrophysics. It was a great setup for me, since I was interested in all kinds of subjects. My dad thinks I spread myself too thin sometimes, but I just enjoy learning, no matter the topic. At the moment, though, I wasn't enjoying learning how to deal with Andrew following my every move.

"Come on," I finally said to Andrew as we filed out of third period. "I'll show you where the cafeteria is." Then I led the way to the second floor.

"So, do you and your friends sit at a special table or something?"

I shrugged. "Yeah, I guess so. I mean, if no one else is sitting there."

"If no one else is sitting there?" he repeated. "They don't hold it for you?"

I stopped and spun around. "Why would anyone hold a table for me?"

Andrew raised his eyebrows. "You know . . . because it's *your* school."

I shook my head, confused. "Yeah, so? Apparently, it's your school now too."

"No, doofus. Because you're Tom Swift. Hello? At the Swift Academy?"

It took a second for it to hit me, and when it did, I let out a moan and rolled my eyes. *That's* why Andrew had made a point of saying he was my friend all morning. He thought I got the royal treatment just because my dad had founded the school.

"No, Andrew," I replied, shaking my head. "I don't get special privileges or anything. I'm a regular student, just like everyone else. And that's how I like it."

Andrew laughed. "Why would you want that?"

"Why would I want people constantly trying to get me to put in a good word with my dad or the principal for every little thing?" I countered, my lips tightening as I pointed at him. "Why would I want people trying to be my friend just to get special treatment?"

Andrew shrugged, unfazed. "Sounds pretty sweet to me. My dad was a major donor at Bradley, so I practically ran the place."

"Huh," I said with a nod. "And now you're here." With that, I spun around and entered the cafeteria.

I got in line, grabbed a tray of food, and headed over to our usual table. Yes, we had a usual table, but it's not like it was behind velvet ropes or anything. I guess we're all just creatures of habit. Noah, Amy, and Sam were already there.

"There he is," Noah said before he popped a tater tot into his mouth. "Where's your oldest and dearest friend?"

I jutted a thumb over my shoulder. "He's here somewhere."

"I hear you two go *way back*," Sam added with a smirk.

"You caught that, huh?"

"Along with everyone else, apparently," she replied. "There's always buzz when there's a new kid in school," she explained. "Especially when it's someone who sabotaged everyone's inventions."

My sporkful of corn froze in front of my mouth. "Yeah, why were you so nice to him this morning?"

"Amy gave me a heads-up that he was here, so I wasn't surprised when he walked into class." A devious grin stretched across Sam's lips. "Besides, I'm just biding my time, Swift. That prank on Amy gave me all kinds of ideas."

Okay, that avenue was definitely worth exploring. By then, I had completely forgotten about Amy's elevator incident. Amy had a way of letting her dark hair curtain her off from the outside world when she was particularly embarrassed. I had failed to notice that she sat at the table a little more curtained than usual.

"How are you holding up?" I asked her.

She sighed and glanced around. "Everyone wants to talk to me about it."

"Well, if it makes you feel any better, I don't think you were a target," I theorized. "I bet it was set for the first person to push the door button."

The elevator gag was far from the first prank pulled at the academy. If you get a bunch of intelligent kids who like inventing under one roof, it's bound to happen. People are *still* talking about Anya Latke's *cat*astrophe prank. A while back, she programmed every computer tied to the school server to play funny cat videos for an hour. Some kids are predicting another *cat*mageddon any day now.

"Yeah, Ames," Noah agreed. "You were just, you know, lucky!"

Amy glared at him and shook her head. Then her

expression softened. "The worst part is"—she looked around again—"I'm still finding confetti ... everywhere."

The four of us stared at one another in silence before we all burst out laughing. Even Amy's shoulders bobbed up and down while her hair completely covered her face.

As I was trying to catch my breath, Noah held up his phone, where his screen showed a shaky video clip of Amy's confetti dump. "I think you're going to have to get used to celebrity status for a while. A bunch of people posted video of you on their blogs."

Amy groaned.

Not so long ago, a production company tried to film a reality show at our school. That didn't go so well, but it inspired a bunch of students to create their own video channels and blogs. Since everyone had their phones at the ready to film all the unusual things at the academy, there was plenty of content to go around.

"Don't worry, Amy," Sam said. "I won't put you on *my* blog."

In my opinion, Sam's blog was one of the best. She did a lot more than just show video clips from around school. She interviewed students, talked about their inventions—all kinds of cool stuff.

"That's hilarious," Andrew said as he peeked over Noah's shoulder at the video. "I didn't get a good look this morning. You gotta send me that link."

Suddenly, lunch didn't taste so good.

"Andrew," I said. "You remember Sam and Amy."

Noah popped another tot into his mouth and leaned back. "You know. Sam? The one who caught the blame for all those sabotaged inventions at camp?"

Amy glared at Andrew while Sam's eyes lit up. She patted the empty seat beside her. "Why don't you join us for lunch?"

"Uh, thanks." He eyed her doubtfully as he eased into the chair and set down his tray. He started to take a bite then stopped. "Okay, okay. I'm *sorry* about the whole camp thing. We were just messing around, you know?"

And the award for least sincere apology goes to . . .

Sam gave a giggle unlike any I'd ever heard her make before. Noah actually jumped a little, startled by the sound.

"Oh, that's all right," she said, playfully nudging Andrew's shoulder. "A vindictive person might want revenge and make your life miserable at your new school. Maybe even save the biggest prank of all just for you."

She shook her head. "But I'm not one to hold a grudge."

That wasn't true. Sam was *totally* one to hold a grudge.

"Uh, okay," Andrew muttered. "Thanks." He slowly twirled his food with his spork. It looked as if he'd lost his appetite.

I tried to hide my smile as I took another bite. Suddenly, my lunch tasted delicious.

4

The Problematic Proposal

I WALKED STIFFLY TO THE BACK OF THE WEIGHT machine and moved the pin down one notch, adding five more kilograms to the load. After making a note of the total weight in my notebook (one hundred kilograms), I clomped back to the bench.

My dad had been working late in his office ever since we got home. He'd been on the phone most of the ride back. Ever since my mother died, Dad has done his best to be two parents in one, but running a big tech company like Swift Enterprises takes up a lot of his time. I didn't mind, though. I didn't have to eat dinner alone very often, and after I finished my homework, I had time to test my latest invention in our home gym.

That was the reason I was so stiff. I'd built a special exoskeleton for my legs. The frame began with two metal cups for my feet, extended up the outside of both legs, and ended at two thick metal belts wrapped snugly around my waist. The flat steel running up my legs was covered with motors, gears, springs, and pulleys. Wires snaked up to battery packs on my waist.

I sat down on the bench, grabbed a handle with each hand, and placed my feet on the inverted platform. Then I extended my legs, pushing the platform away. Cables ran from the platform, up to a pulley, and down to the stack of heavy weights, where the pressure from my feet caused the weights to rise into the air.

Without the exoskeleton, one hundred kilograms was about all I could leg press. But *with* the exoskeleton, I could press that much weight without breaking a sweat.

Pressure meters on the soles of my feet (actually track pads salvaged from a couple of old laptops) measured how much pressure I exerted and ramped up the motors to help with the load. I knew I wasn't the first one to come up with this idea, but I'm hoping that my prototype will lead to a device that can help rehabilitate someone with an injury, or even help someone walk again.

Thrilled with the results, I sprung off the bench and moved the pin down two more notches. I added the total weight to my notebook (one hundred and ten kilograms) and took my position on the bench again.

With only a little more effort on my part, the load went up and down like before.

Perfect.

I hopped off the bench and added another ten kilograms, made a note, and got back in position.

"Tom?" my dad called from the hallway.

"In here," I replied, getting my feet back in position.

My dad's eyes lit up when he came into the gym and saw what I was up to. "Testing the new bionic legs, huh?"

That was his name for them, not mine. He said it had something to do with an old TV show about a guy who had robotic body parts and fought crime, or something weird like that.

"I have it set for a hundred and twenty kilograms," I told him.

My dad whistled. "That's almost two hundred and sixty-five pounds."

"Check it," I said as I pushed against the platform. This time, I could definitely feel the weight, but the motors whined, and the weights lifted just as before.

My father raised an eyebrow. "Impressive."

PING!

Something snapped off my right leg brace. The motors whirred louder, and I suddenly felt the full weight with my right leg. "Uh-oh," was all I could get out before the platform slammed down to its resting place. The force pushed me back, making me slide down the bench.

My dad raced over. "Are you all right?"

"I'm fine." I was startled, but otherwise okay. I glanced around the room. "I think I popped a spring or something." I didn't see it anywhere. Glancing up at my father, I said, "I guess it's back to the drawing board." It was another phrase he always used.

"And what did you learn?"

I shrugged. "I need stronger springs, maybe?" I would have to go over the braces to be sure all the components could handle a bigger load.

"You might think about beefing up those motors, too," he suggested. "One of them sounded strained near the end there."

"Good idea." With a sigh, I gave up my search for the missing spring, scooped up my notebook, and limped toward the door. I wasn't injured, but with one leg brace out of commission, the other one had me off balance with too much bounce in my step.

"Oh, Tom," Dad said. "I didn't get a chance to talk to you about the new student at school."

I stopped and turned around. "You heard about that, huh?" My dad didn't know about everything that went on at the school, but he kept up with the important stuff. Or in this case, the things that affected me personally.

"Your principal wanted my opinion on whether or not to let Andrew enroll," he explained. "Especially after what he pulled at camp."

I shook my head. "Yeah, I can't believe he got in after that."

"Oh, Davenport was against it," my father said. "But I talked him into it."

My eyes felt like they were going to bug out of my skull. "You what!"

"Well, I didn't literally talk him into it," my dad explained. "I just put in a good word. It was ultimately your principal's decision."

"But why?" I asked. "You remember what he was like when we were little?"

"You two were fast friends once."

That was true. We had started off as friends, but near the end, Andrew had become more of a bully. "Remember how he'd get me in trouble all the time?"

My dad smirked. "Don't you think you should take some responsibility on that front?"

"Well, maybe," I said. "But he always has something rotten to say about everything, and I mean everything. Unless he's talking about himself, of course. Then it's all wonderful."

My dad crossed his arms. "I'll tell you what I told your principal: Everyone deserves a second chance."

"Really? Andrew?"

My dad sat on the bench press machine. "Let me give you another example. How do you like Mitchell Osborne?"

"Our new chemistry teacher?" I asked. "He seems all right." I didn't have the heart to tell my dad how we scared him this morning with our robot.

"Well, up until a week ago, he was one of my researchers. He's very smart, but he just wasn't working out."

"Why?"

"That doesn't matter." My father waved off the question. "But what does is that Osborne has a family to support, and I thought a good second chance would be working at the academy."

My shoulders slumped. "But Andrew Foger? Really?"

My dad stood and put a hand on my shoulder. "Have you ever wondered why he acts the way he does? My guess is he's a pretty insecure guy. Add that to being the new kid at school." My dad shrugged. "He could probably use a friend."

"Oh, he's tried that." I explained how Andrew had been telling everyone he and I were best buds.

My father laughed. "Yup. Sounds insecure to me. Why don't you help him out? Give him a second chance?"

I let out a long sigh. "I'll try."

After that, I went to my room, stripped off my exoskeleton, and plopped down in front of my computer. I knew that even if I gave Andrew another shot, there was no way Sam would do the same. If I was being honest, I kind of felt bad for the guy. It hadn't been my dad's talk that swayed me. It was knowing that Sam had something big planned.

Thinking of her, I clicked over to her blog to see if she'd posted another video. She hadn't. Then I searched for video of Amy in the elevator. Just as Noah had predicted, she was on several students' channels. I watched confetti dumping on her from every angle. She was going to be famous for a while, all right.

My search turned up a blog that I hadn't heard of before called the *Not-So-Swift Academy*. I wasn't a fan of the name, but still hit play on the one and only video posted there, and was greeted by a host with a blurred-out face. The person was shot from the waist up and sat in front of an animated background. The blogger must have put up a green screen, then projected what looked like a screen saver featuring dozens of falling squares.

"The Swift Academy is supposed to be filled with some of the best and brightest," the host said in a deep, digitally camouflaged voice. "Let's take a look, shall we?"

The video cut to a tightly edited montage of all the camera angles of the prank on Amy. There were even silly sound effects—boings, buzzes, and whirs accompanied every confetti drop as Amy was showered over and over and over again. The assembled clips took a simple prank and presented it in a vicious way.

The video cut back to the blogger laughing. "Subscribe to my blog for more examples of educational excellence from the Not-So-Swift Academy!"

As the video ended, I couldn't help concluding one thing: Amy was going to be devastated.

5

The Olfactory Offensive

WHEN I ARRIVED AT SCHOOL THE NEXT MORNING,
I wondered if Amy had seen or heard about the video. I
had thought about shooting her a text the night before,
but why ruin her night if she hadn't, right?

My question was answered as soon as I stepped
into algebra. Sam and Amy were already there. I
assumed it was Amy. The person sitting at her desk
was wearing a hooded sweater, its hood bound tightly
around her head.

"So, I guess you saw the video, huh?" I asked as I slid
into my desk.

"Tell her that the hood only draws more attention to her," Sam insisted.

I spun back to look at Amy. Her nose was all that jutted from the cinched hood. "She has a point, you know."

Amy sighed and cautiously pulled the hood back from her face. "I guess you're right."

Just then, Noah plopped his backpack down and slid into his desk to join us. "Oh, man. Did you guys see that vid—" My best friend shut his mouth when he realized the three of us were staring back at him. "Oh. I guess you did."

Sam glared at him. "I've been trying to tell Amy that it's really no big deal."

"She's right, Ames," Noah agreed quickly. "People get pranked all the time. Everyone will forget the whole thing in two, three days, tops."

Amy sunk lower in her seat. "Three days?"

"Sit up, Amy," Sam ordered. "Whoever did this, you can't let them see it getting to you. That's what they want. You just have to brush it off like it's no big deal."

Amy nodded and sat straighter. "You're right." She sucked in a deep breath. "It's no big deal."

"There she is," Andrew said loudly as he strolled in. "Confetti girl!"

When the classroom broke out in a burst of laughter, Amy squeaked and pulled the hood back over her head.

I couldn't see it, but I imagined the thunderous look Sam had shot Andrew. I could see his reaction, though—he stiffened and quickly looked away, rushing to his seat in the back of the classroom.

Sam slowly spun around, her lips screwed into a scowl. "I don't know what I'm going to do to him yet, but it's going to be big."

For the second time in two days, I felt kind of sorry for Andrew Foger. It must've been a new record.

I don't know if it was Sam's look or the fact that being my friend wasn't going to get him any special privileges, but unlike the day before, Andrew kept his distance throughout the day. He didn't speak to me in any classes and he was nowhere to be found during lunch.

I was grateful for the break, but it also made me think more about what my father had said the night before. Even if Andrew was a huge pain, it must be hard being alone in a new school without any friends. I guessed I could be a little nicer to him.

How hard could it be?

I made a point of catching him as we left physics. "So—" I began.

"Oh, hey, Junior," he interrupted. "I forgot to tell you. Wait till you see the surprise I have for you in robotics."

"Oh, yeah?" Talking about new inventions was always a great way to break the ice. "What is it?"

Andrew gave an exaggerated nod. "That's for me to know and you to find out." He ended with a loud guffaw.

That was the same dumb line he used to give me when we were kids. It was always his way of boasting how he knew something that I didn't.

"Whatever," I said, then turned toward my locker.

Okay, being nicer to him was going to be harder than I thought.

After I grabbed some spare parts from my locker, I caught up with Noah in the stairwell to the third floor. "Did you get to finish the update last night?" I asked him.

"Yep," he replied with a grin. "I dialed down Raider's flight response, so no worries there. I also added some surprises I think you'll like."

"Cool!"

When we got to the robotics lab, everyone was crowded into one corner looking down at the floor.

Almost everyone. Sam sat at our worktable with her back to the others.

She jutted a thumb over her shoulder. "You're going to love this one, Swift."

Noah and I set our backpacks on the table before joining the circle. It wasn't uncommon to come upon scenes like this in robotics. Folks were thrilled to witness a student's new invention, especially if it was a robot. Judging from the way everyone was laughing, this one must've been good. I was excited as Noah and I pushed into the crowd for a look.

That excitement was quickly dashed when I saw what had my classmates so worked up. Andrew was crouched there, showing off his robot.

He noticed me at once. "You're just in time, Junior. I told you I'd already built a dog robot."

Andrew's "dog" robot was actually a modified Star Wars toy. You know, one of those Imperial walkers? Well, it looked as if Andrew had mechanized it so it could walk around on its own. He'd even added two floppy ears and a segmented tail on the back.

"Check it," Andrew said, before turning back to the robot. "Sit!"

The walker folded its hind legs and its rump landed on the floor. The other students giggled and clapped.

"Down," Andrew ordered.

The walker pushed its front legs out until it looked like a little robot dog, eagerly waiting for its next command.

"Good boy," Andrew cooed.

The segmented tail wagged back and forth.

"That's my favorite part," Jamal Watts said with a laugh.

I'd seen enough. I backed out of the crowd, Noah close on my heels, and rejoined Sam at the worktable. "So, you were being sarcastic when you said I would love it."

Sam shrugged. "Well, yeah. Can't you tell by now?"

"No," Noah and I said in unison.

"Too bad." Sam smirked as she went back to oiling one of Raider's wheels. She'd been a big help with robot maintenance, especially after the confetti incident.

Noah pulled his laptop out of his backpack. "You know they already make toy dog robots that can do all the stuff Andrew's can, right?" He opened his computer and turned it on, then leaned closer. "I think that little tail is actually from one of those toys."

"It probably was," I agreed. Then I sighed, remembering what my dad had said about second chances. "But . . . it must've been difficult to retrofit it onto an Imperial walker."

"It's an AT-AT, to be precise," Sam chimed in. "All Terrain Armored Transport. Not to be confused with the new AT-M6 that—"

Noah rolled his eyes. "We get it. You're a fan."

Sam simply smiled as she greased another wheel. She was a huge science fiction fan. She could not only name all the Star Wars vehicles, but knew all the alien species, what planets they were from . . . It was crazy impressive.

Noah leaned in again. "And why are you taking his side anyway?"

I raised both hands. "I'm not. I'm just saying—"

"What do you think, Junior?" Andrew asked as he set his robot on our worktable. "Voice recognition and everything."

"That's a pretty cool design," I admitted.

"Yeah, we'll have voice recognition as soon as I install this update," Noah explained as he tapped away on his laptop.

Andrew leaned in for a closer look. "You forgot to hook it up, genius."

Noah reached over and flicked Raider's antenna tail. "Wi-Fi."

"Oh," Andrew scoffed.

Noah tapped a few more keys. "And . . . done." He closed his laptop and leaned back. "Raider, where's Tom?"

The robot rotated until he faced me. "Hello, Tom," came a robotic voice from a tiny speaker in front.

I laughed. "That's so cool."

"I added facial recognition last night," Noah explained. "Raider, where's Sam?"

The robot rotated again until he came face-to-face with Sam. "Hello, Sam."

"Wow," she said. "Way to go!"

"Not bad," said Andrew. "Do me next."

"I didn't program your face, but . . ." Noah spun the robot to face himself and then motioned Andrew closer. Andrew leaned in. "Raider, this is Andy."

Andrew jumped back. "My name is Andrew."

"Raider, find Andy," Noah instructed.

The robot rotated, tracking Andrew's movements. "Hello, Andy," he said.

We laughed as Andrew tried to move out of Raider's line of sight. "It's Andrew," he repeated with a scowl.

"Hello, Andy," Raider called again.

Andrew shook his head as he scooped up his robot and moved to one of the other worktables.

Noah leaned over to me. "I thought you'd appreciate that . . . Junior."

I laughed harder. "You don't know how much."

The rest of the class period flew by as the three of us made more adjustments to Raider. It turned out that Noah had added another surprise to our robot—an invisible leash. It was a small transmitter that clipped to a person's belt. Raider would follow whoever wore it. I got to be the one to test it and it worked like a charm. When I left the classroom, Raider obediently followed me down the hall toward the elevator. Again, it was no big deal to see a robot following a student through the halls at Swift Academy. Noah told me he'd gotten the idea from Jessie Steele and her book bag on wheels that followed her wherever she went.

Raider and I boarded the elevator with a couple of other students and headed down to the first floor. However, when the elevator stopped at the second floor, screams echoed from the adjacent hallway.

As we bolted from the elevator to see what was going

on, I heard our robot's motor behind me, so I knew the invisible leash was still working. I skidded to a stop in front of the biology classroom along with everyone else. Students scrambled out the door, followed by dozens of white rats!

Some students laughed, recording the debacle on their phones, while others recoiled in disgust. Jim Mills was one of the laughers. He stepped forward and scooped up a rodent.

"Hey, it's just a toy," he announced.

As soon as he said it, I noticed the faint whirring sounds of tiny motors underneath all the laughter and squealing.

Jim shook the mechanical rat and a small glass vial fell out and smashed against the floor, leaving a pool of liquid among the tiny shards. I was close to Jim, so the smell hit me like a slap to the face. My nostrils were assaulted by the sulfurous tang of rotten eggs.

"Stink bomb." I barely got out the words before I was pushing my way back through the crowd.

Turns out, I didn't need to say anything. Students coughed and gagged as the pungent vapor cloud expanded. The hallway cleared in record time.

6

The Disconcerting Incursion

"OKAY, RAIDER," NOAH SAID. "FIND TOM."

The robot spun in a circle until he faced Sam. She held out her phone, recording the entire thing. Raider spun a little more until he faced Amy, pausing on her for a moment before rotating again. He paused again when he was facing in my direction. I was thirty meters down the track, so the robot's motor whirred as he closed the distance. When he finally reached me, he stopped and angled his head up to my face.

"Hello, Tom," Raider greeted through his electronic voice.

"Very nice," Sam said, still recording.

The four of us had gotten together after school. Sam wanted to feature our robot on her blog, and the academy's large running track was the perfect place to put Raider through his paces. Since Noah had worked most of the bugs out of the robot's programming, we were finally ready to show him off.

I still had the invisible leash clipped to my belt, so Raider obediently followed me as I walked back to my friends.

"And since Raider has his own AI, he can add other faces to his facial recognition database," Noah explained, mugging for the camera a little. My best friend wasn't camera shy by any means.

In contrast, Amy was silent, standing just out of frame as Sam recorded the robot and us. Amy was a whiz at editing and animating, so she was happiest working behind the scenes.

"What else can he do?" Sam asked, aiming the camera back at Raider.

"This is a cool one," I said, leaning over the robot. "Raider, patrol."

His motors whined as he sped off. When he was

about ten meters away, he began to circle our group in a slow arc, pausing every five meters to turn away from us, scanning for threats.

Sam recorded Raider's actions for a bit before aiming her phone back at me. "So, I heard you saw the rat prank firsthand today."

"I thought this was about our robot," I replied.

Sam shrugged. "I report on all Swift Academy activity." The camera lens remained focused on me.

Noah jumped into frame. "I wish I could've seen it. It sounded hilarious."

I waved my hand in front of my nose. "Not if you'd smelled it." The stench still lingered as if part of it was stuck in my nose.

"Was it as bad as Stinky's fiasco?" Sam asked.

I laughed. "No way."

Last year, Steve Krieger had a chemistry mishap that reeked so bad, it had cleared the entire second floor of the academy. And so his new nickname was born— Stinky.

Sam switched her phone to selfie mode. Amy squeaked, quickly ducking out of frame. "Who could be behind these pranks at our school?" Sam asked the camera. "Who is the blurred blogger on the *Not-So-Swift Academy* blog? Someone with a grudge against the school, maybe? An outsider, perhaps?"

Sam was always interested in a good conspiracy theory, but I could see where this one was going.

"Can you cut a minute?" I asked.

She tapped her screen to stop recording. "Sure, what's wrong?"

"So, is this how you're going to get back at Andrew?" I asked. "Make everyone think he's the blurred blogger?"

"Oh, yeah," Noah said. "That's a good one, Sam."

"Who says I'm getting back at him?" she asked. "What if he really is the one behind the pranks?"

"They *did* start the day he arrived," Amy chimed in.

I shook my head. "Yeah, but how could he have set up that elevator prank on his first day of school? That doesn't make any sense."

"Ah!" Sam raised a finger. "But what if the prankster and the blurred blogger are two different people?"

"Hey, that's a thought," Noah said. Then his brow furrowed. "Wait, why is that a thought?"

"Because the blogger could've just used the footage from everyone's phones," Sam replied.

"That's true." Amy nodded, then glanced down and shifted uncomfortably. "It seems like everyone uploaded the footage to their video channels."

I had to admit it—Sam had a good point. There were a bunch of free programs out there that let users save videos from websites—I had a couple myself. Even the simplest editing programs could have cut together the montage of Amy getting covered in confetti. And the blogger seemed to have it out for Swift Academy. It sounded like something Andrew could've done.

"But why would he dump on a school he was attending?" I asked.

Sam's eyes lit up. "Maybe he's a spy. What if he's just here for a couple of weeks before going back to Bradley?"

I thought of the expression I'd seen on Andrew's face when I'd made that dig about him not being at Bradley anymore. I had a feeling there was more to that story.

After a beat, I let out a long sigh. "My dad says I should give him a second chance."

"What?!" my friends said in unison.

"After what he did to everyone's projects?" Sam asked. "After what he did to me?"

Amy crossed her arms. "I'm surprised that anyone in this school is even talking to him."

I laughed nervously. "I know, right?"

I wanted to take my dad's advice. I usually did. But my friends had a point. How could any of us ever trust Andrew again? Then again, he and I had been friends once. I don't know why he slowly morphed into a bully, but maybe there had been a reason. Maybe if I gave him a second chance, I could find out.

Raider halted his patrol and scooted back to us. "Hello, Tom," he said as he stopped in front of me.

"Did you tell Raider to stop?" I asked Noah.

Noah crouched beside the robot. "No, I didn't."

Raider spun to face Noah. "Hello, Noah," he greeted. "Tom Swift sleeps with a teddy bear."

Noah burst into laughter. "What was that?"

Raider turned to face Amy and Sam. "Tom Swift sleeps with a teddy bear."

Amy gasped, while Sam slowly raised her phone, ready to record.

I pointed to her, glaring. "Don't you dare."

"Tom Swift sleeps with a teddy bear," Raider repeated. "Tom Swift sleeps with a teddy bear."

With lightning speed, I reached down and flicked the robot's kill switch. Raider went silent before he could get another word out.

"First of all, I do *not* sleep with a teddy bear," I insisted. "And even if I did, how could he know? Raider has never been in my room. I've only worked on him in the garage."

My three friends exchanged glances before completely losing it.

I nodded at Noah. "Did you make Raider say that?"

Noah shook his head, managing a straight face only long enough to get out, "Not me, man. I'll have to check the program tonight."

I hadn't been lying. I didn't sleep with a teddy bear. At least, not since I was a little. . . .

I shot to my feet and glanced around. The school grounds were mostly empty, but there were a few students here and there. Some were reading books while others seemed to be working on inventions of their own. None of them had their attention on me or my cackling friends.

I shifted my gaze to the school itself, spotting a student peering down from a third-floor window. He ducked out of sight when he saw me looking, but not before I could make out who it was—none other than Andrew Foger.

My face flushed with anger. This kid was making it really hard to follow my dad's advice.

7

The Pigment Infringement

"ALL RIGHT, GANG." MR. OSBORNE SLAPPED A large ice chest on his desk. "Can anyone tell me why I had to drive with the windows down when I brought this thing to school today?"

I raised my hand, along with a few other students. Mr. Osborne pointed to Evan Wittman.

"Because of the carbon dioxide?" Evan asked.

Mr. Osborne slapped the cooler again. "Correct. As you all know, dry ice is frozen carbon dioxide. And if it's in an environment above minus seventy-eight degrees Celsius, it sublimates, or moves directly from solid to gaseous form." He pointed to himself. "And since I'm human and breathe oxygen, expelling CO_2, with the windows up, I could've passed out and plowed into a tree."

I glanced over to Andrew's worktable. Same as the rest of the morning, he didn't look my way.

As far as my friends were concerned, Andrew was definitely either the prankster, the blogger, or both. Our hacked robot was all the proof they needed. I wasn't one hundred percent convinced about the other pranks, but I was furious he'd hacked Raider, and I was relieved that no one had been around to record the hijacked bot. If there was no footage, then at least I wouldn't be on the next episode of the *Not-So-Swift Academy*. I hoped that was the case, anyway. Noah didn't think Andrew could access Raider's eye cameras when he hacked in, but either way, my best friend vowed to beef up security so it wouldn't happen again.

That day, I'd arrived at school with a mission: I was going to confront Andrew to see if I could get him to come clean.

"Safety glasses on," Mr. Osborne instructed. "I'm going to pass out dry ice pellets so you can see sublimation up close." He began moving about the lab, using tongs to place a couple of pellets onto flat trays on our worktables. "Use your tongs to place the dry ice inside the rubber gloves I gave each group. Then tie off the gloves like a balloon."

Amy was my lab partner as usual, and she got to work as soon as we'd received our pellets. After we'd each tied off the dry ice in our glove, the rubber hands began to expand.

I felt my phone vibrate in my pocket and pulled it out. Noah had sent me a link. I tapped it to see that another video had been uploaded by the blurred blogger.

"Check it," I murmured to Amy, carefully holding my phone below the worktable's surface so I wouldn't get busted for being on it during class.

I had the volume down, so we couldn't hear the blogger's creepy deep voice, though I was surprised to see that the mystery host was in front of another animated background, this one filled with floating poop emojis. After a few moments, the video cut to a camera angle inside the biology lab. Students began to rise and gather their things—Mrs. Livingston must've just dismissed class.

"Look," Amy said, pointing to the top of the screen.

In the back of the classroom, a panel under one of the cabinets flopped down and dozens of white rats poured out of the opening. Even though I knew they were just mechanical rodents, they looked very real on my screen. My guess was they seemed real in person too; in the video students were screaming and scattering as the rats spread out across the room.

The feed cut to a camera angle from the hallway outside the biology classroom. The view was focused for a moment on a closed door before it flew open. Students streamed out followed by a swarm of rats.

Pop!

Back in our classroom, someone's glove had popped as the dry ice sublimated. Several students laughed, and a few covered their ears, waiting for their own gloves to pop.

I turned my attention back to the video, which showed the action from another camera angle. I even saw myself run into view. I watched all over again as Jim picked up one of the toy rats, and then dropped it when he noticed its stinky surprise.

Pop! Pop-pop-pop!

Amy didn't seem fazed by the exploding gloves. She grabbed my phone and slid back the progress bar. "Did you see that?" she asked as the view returned to the interior of the classroom. "This wasn't shot from a phone. Look at the camera angle."

Sure enough, the interior of the classroom was being shown from above, as if the camera were mounted high on the wall. Of course Amy and all her editing skills would notice a detail everyone else takes for granted— the camera angle.

"The academy has security cameras inside the classrooms?" I glanced around the chem lab, but I didn't see any. I knew the school had cameras in the hallways, but not inside the classrooms.

Amy looked around too. "Maybe it's just some of the classrooms?"

Pop! Pop!

We barely noticed as both of our gloves blew; we were too focused on the rewound video footage. As before, it had cut to the scene from out in the hallway. I hadn't noticed it the first time, but now I processed that the scene was shot from two cameras, both of which appeared to be mounted high up on the wall.

"Whoever uploaded this hacked the school security system?" I asked.

Amy shrugged. "Looks like it."

I glanced over at Andrew. His focus was on his inflating glove. I knew he'd hacked Raider, so maybe he was skilled enough to hack into the school's system too.

As most of the gloves had blown, Mr. Osborne dragged a large plastic trash can to the front of the class. "Remember what I said yesterday about expanding gases in confined spaces? Well, I have another demonstration for you."

The teacher unscrewed the cap from a half-drunk water bottle. He took a long sip before grabbing another dry ice pellet with a pair of tongs and then dropped the chunk into the bottle. The remaining water began to bubble, and a light fog wafted out of the opening, drifting toward the floor.

"You might see this effect in haunted houses or old movies," Mr. Osborne explained. "You get even more fog when the water is heated." He screwed the cap back on and held the bottle over the trash can with a pair of tongs. "Now, as I've said at the beginning of most of these experiments, don't try this at home."

I lost interest in Andrew and the video. Along with the rest of the class, I watched as the plastic bottle slowly expanded, making crinkling sounds. The ridges and indentations smoothed out and then the plastic label popped off.

"That ought to do it," Mr. Osborne said as he

dropped the bottle into the trash. He took a step to the side and held up a finger. "Wait for it. . . ."

Everyone was silent, their attention fixed on the front of the room.

POW!

My classmates jumped before breaking into excited conversation. Some kids even applauded.

"Okay, gang," Mr. Osborne said, raising his hands. "Grab some glassware, thermometers, scales, and dry ice. I want rates of sublimation at various temperatures." We all rose from our stools, heading for the supply closet and the ice chest. "Tongs and safety glasses," Mr. Osborne said sternly. "And no sealed containers. Oh, and let's get some windows open. Can't have you passing out while you run your tests."

There was a smattering of laughter as I joined a couple of other students in opening the windows. The chemistry lab was one of the few classrooms where the windows did open, angling out to let in fresh air. Although that hadn't really helped much during Stinky's experiment.

While everyone was away from their worktables, I seized the opportunity to talk to Andrew. I caught him as he was coming back with supplies.

"Was it you?" I demanded.

"Was what me?" he asked back.

I crossed my arms. "The pranks. Hacking Raider. The *Not-So-Swift* blog?"

"I don't know what you're talking about."

He tried to push past me, but I held my ground. "It sounds like something you'd do. Anything to make the school look bad."

Andrew rolled his eyes. "Hello?" he said, tapping my chest with a thermometer. "Anybody home, Junior? It's my school too now."

I pushed his hand away and narrowed my eyes. "Yeah, and why is that?"

Andrew's lips tightened. "*That's* none of your business."

"I bet you're here just long enough to sabotage us again. You'll probably be back at Bradley as soon as you get enough pranks to broadcast on your stupid blog."

"Is that your weak theory, Sherlock?" Andrew asked with a laugh.

"What are you going to do? Make it look like Sam was behind everything just like you did at camp?"

"I *said* I was sorry, Junior."

My face flushed with rage. "Stop calling me that!"

"You fellas want to get back to work and take a trip down memory lane some other time?" Mr. Osborne asked. He had a grip on each of our shoulders. I hadn't even seen him walk up behind us. "I haven't sent anyone to the principal's office yet, and I would hate to start with you two."

I let out a long sigh. "Sorry. We're fine."

As I returned to my worktable, I was surprised to see the rest of the class eyeing Andrew and me. Luckily, Amy had gathered all our supplies, so I could bury my embarrassment in focusing on our assignment.

"That looked a little . . . intense," Amy observed.

"Yeah. Andrew denied everything," I said as I lit the Bunsen burner and began heating our beaker of water.

I tried to forget about Andrew and just concentrate on the steps of the experiment. Amy and I recorded temperatures, weighed dry ice pellets, and did our best to come up with the requested data. I must say, with all the bubbling and smoking beakers, the place looked more like a mad scientist's lab than usual.

When class was over, Andrew ducked out before Amy and I had finished putting away our supplies. I thought about asking Amy to cover for me again so I could catch up with him, but then changed my mind.

What was the use? He would just deny everything like he did before.

As we were leaving the classroom, a loud alarm blared. Our school had had fire drills in the past, but this one was nothing like those. The deafening repetitive buzzing sounded as if the school was having a nuclear meltdown or something.

Amy and I ran up the hall to find dozens of students standing in a wide semicircle around one of the walls. Most of them had their hands clamped over their ears.

I spotted Noah and ran up to him. "What is that?!" I shouted, trying to block out the racket.

Noah pointed to a box mounted on the wall. It was about twelve centimeters wide and had a comically large red button sticking out from the front. Big white letters printed across the button read DO NOT PUSH.

"This is what happened when someone pushed that?" Amy shouted.

Noah nodded.

I glanced around, half expecting steel doors to slam shut around us as the entire school went on lockdown. Instead, I saw classmates laughing and covering their ears. Apparently, the blaring alarm was punishment enough.

"Has anyone tried pushing it again?" I asked.

"I did!" Noah called over the racket. "Right after I pushed it the first time!"

My jaw dropped. "Wait, *you* pushed it?!"

Noah shrugged. "Well . . . yeah."

"Why?"

Noah waved toward the wall. "Because it said not to."

"Don't you think that's why you *shouldn't* have pushed it?" Amy asked.

Noah rolled his eyes. "Something like that pops up in plain view, you have to see what it does."

The guy had a point. In a school full of curious kids, someone was bound to push it sooner or later. If it hadn't been Noah, it would have been someone else.

"Well, are you satisfied now?" I cried over the deafening buzz.

Noah shook his head. "Not so much, no."

"How do you shut it off?!" Amy shouted.

Holding my ears tighter, I moved closer to the box. Noah peered over my shoulder as I leaned in. There were no wires or conduit leading to it.

"Maybe the battery will run out," I suggested weakly. But that didn't seem to sit well with Noah. "That's it," he cried, grabbing it on either side and giving it a big yank. Nothing happened. He leaned forward and examined the box again before turning back to the gathered students. "Anyone have a screwdriver?"

"I got it," Amy said as she slid off her backpack. Of course Amy had a screwdriver handy. Her backpack put Batman's utility belt to shame. She quickly produced the tool and handed it over.

Noah took the screwdriver and jammed it into a seam on the side of the box. After a few seconds (which felt like an eternity with the blaring alarm assaulting my ears), he managed to pop off the front. He held the cover, following two wires trailing into a mechanism nestled in the other half. With a tug, he jerked the front half free, snapping the thin wires, and the alarm stopped abruptly. Everyone cheered.

Breaking the connection must've cut the power.

Unfortunately, that wasn't the only thing that happened. As Noah leaned in to get a better look at the mechanism, blue liquid squirted out.

"Ack!" Noah sputtered as he got a face full of the stuff.

The cheers of the crowd turned to laughter. The prankster had struck again.

8

The Evidentiary Expedition

"WHAT WAS NOAH THINKING?" SAM ASKED AS she unpacked her lunch. "Especially with all the pranks going on."

I shrugged as I salted my green beans. "To be fair, I probably would've done the same thing."

"No way," Sam said.

Amy opened her container of pasta and grinned. "It was a very enticing button."

Sam laughed. "You too, Amy?"

"Well, I wouldn't have pushed it," Amy replied. "But I can definitely see the appeal."

Sam took a bite of her sandwich and nodded at me. "Deena Bittick told me about your blowup with Andrew Foger today."

I winced. News sure traveled fast around our school. Deena wasn't even in our chemistry class.

"Thanks for standing up for me, Swift," Sam continued. "And just so you know, word is getting around that Andrew is the prankster." She gave a devious grin. "I may not have to get him back after all, thanks to you."

I felt a pang of guilt. Sure, I was 99 percent positive Andrew was the prankster, and I admit I wasn't his biggest fan, but I didn't mean to start a rumor about the guy. Besides, Sam should know better than anyone that starting rumors was never a good idea. It was partly my fault that she'd been blamed for Andrew's last attack on our school.

"I didn't realize the entire class and Mr. Osborne were listening," I explained.

Sam opened her mouth to answer, but was interrupted by Noah slamming his tray down onto the table.

"I don't want to hear it," he said.

I glanced up to see that most of my best friend's face

was stained dark blue. So the three of us did what you'd expect if one of your friends found himself in a similar predicament: We burst out laughing.

Noah shook his head and threw himself into the chair. "Go ahead. Get it over with. But if I hear one more Smurf joke, I'm going to break something."

"That many, huh?" I asked.

Noah began counting on his fingers. "Barry Jacobs, Alicia Wilkes, Tristan Caudle . . ."

"Did anyone say you're looking a little blue today?" Sam asked, trying to keep it together.

Noah turned to her, wide-eyed. "Yeah! Mr. Wilkins."

The three of us laughed even harder.

Noah rubbed the side of his face. "It won't wash off, you guys. Seriously. I don't know how long I'll be like this. I'm thinking of skipping tomorrow."

"You could quit school altogether and try out for the Blue Man Group," Amy suggested. She barely managed to get out the line before she lost it.

Noah threw his hands up. "Thanks a lot, Ames. No one's used that one yet."

"So I take it you don't think the pranks are funny anymore?" I asked.

Noah pointed to his blue skin. "Does this look like an amused face?"

"It looks like a lack-of-oxygen face," I shot back. That set Amy off again; Sam almost choked on her drink. Noah glared at me across the table.

I held my hands out. "Okay, okay. That was the last one. Promise."

Noah shook his head. "Man, when I get my hands on Andrew. Excuse me . . . *Andy*. I was already mad that he hacked Raider."

"I bet Mr. Davenport will handle everything for you," Sam suggested. She went on to tell how I started the rumor that Andrew was behind everything.

"Oh, man. You did that?" Noah asked. "Toby Nguyen said something about that, but I had no idea you started the story."

I rubbed the back of my neck. "Yeah, me neither."

"Speaking of hacking," Amy interjected. "Tom and I think Andrew hacked into the school's security system too." She told them about the high camera angles we'd seen in the videos on the blurred blogger's page.

Sam popped a piece of fruit into her mouth and grinned as she chewed. "Then Davenport will definitely get him."

As my friends tried to guess what kind of punishment Andrew would get, I thought of those weird camera angles. It still seemed strange that the academy would have cameras in some classrooms and not others. It seemed even odder that I'd never noticed them before. Sure, security cameras were supposed to be unobtrusive, but two cameras so close together outside biology class seemed like overkill. I don't know why, but something about the entire setup really bugged me. And if there was one thing I knew about myself, my subconscious would obsess about this conundrum until I got my questions answered.

I popped a few more tater tots into my mouth before grabbing my tray and standing up. "I'll catch up with you later. I have to check on a few things."

"Can you figure out how to wash off blue dye while you're at it?" Noah said. "I'm asking for a friend."

I chuckled. "You should check with Mr. Osborne. He might know."

Noah's eyes lit up. "Hey, good idea." He began to wolf down his food. "Maybe I can catch him."

I didn't wait for Noah. Instead, I dumped my tray and left the cafeteria, hitting the stairs and heading up to the third floor. When I reached the landing, I glanced up and spotted the security camera mounted above the stairwell entrance. The little black dome no doubt housed a camera with a clear view straight down the hallway, but that wasn't the one I was concerned with, so I kept going down the hall.

When I reached the biology classroom door, it was shut, so I knocked lightly before turning the knob and pushing it open. The room was dark, and Mrs. Livingston was nowhere to be seen. I immediately spotted the open panel I'd seen on the video. The long, thin piece of wood under the cabinet remained flat on the floor after the toy rats had escaped their hiding place.

I spun around to look for the security camera on the opposite wall, but there was nothing there except Mrs. Livingston's posters and infographics. I moved closer—could it be hidden somehow?

Still not seeing anything out of place, I pulled out my phone and pulled up the video. With no one around, I turned up the volume to see what the blurred blogger had to say:

"Did I mention that they teach biology at the Not-So-Swift Academy? Well, check out how these brave students react when a few lab animals stage a mutiny." The video cut to the overhead view. I paused it just as the panel under the cabinet fell open.

Using the frozen frame as a guide, I backed against the wall, trying to put myself in the same place as the camera. When I thought I had it right, I turned back to the wall. There was still nothing there—not even the smallest hole where the tiniest of cameras could have been housed.

After looking around for a few more moments, I stepped out of the classroom, stopping in front of the door to scan the opposite wall for the other two cameras. They were nowhere in sight. I started the video again until it cut to the hallway view. Just as before, I paused the clip and tried to locate the cameras.

They just weren't there.

9

The Admission Analysis

IN PHYSICS, ONCE THE BELL HAD RUNG, SAM nudged my arm. "Check out who didn't make it to class," she whispered.

I followed her gaze to the back of the classroom, confirming that Andrew's desk was empty. When I turned back to my friends, Sam was nodding approvingly, Amy was smiling, and a wide grin stretched across Noah's blue face.

"I *so* bet he got expelled," Noah whispered.

I'm sure they would've loved nothing more than to continue their speculation on what Mr. Davenport was doing to Andrew. Unfortunately, Mrs. Lee didn't allow discussions about non-physics-related subjects. We kept our suspicions about Andrew's absence to ourselves for the rest of the period.

At least Noah, Sam, and I could discuss things openly in our next class—robotics. It was a much more relaxed atmosphere. However, when we got there, Sam, Noah, and I were surprised when Andrew walked through the door just before the tardy bell rang.

I could see shock on Sam's face and anger simmering on Noah's. Bad vibes were flying all around as Andrew glared our way before sitting down at his own worktable.

"Pardon the interruption," Mr. Davenport's voice blared over the school intercom. "As most of you know, our school has been the target of a prankster lately. Now, I know spirits get a little high from time to time, but these pranks are not only beginning to disrupt normal school operation; I've been informed that they're also now involving damage to school property, and we cannot tolerate such behavior."

I glanced at my friends. Sam shrugged, while Noah shook his head. I wondered which prank Mr. Davenport was referring to. The mystery button certainly hadn't been school property.

"I've already questioned a few students," our principal continued, "but I've yet to identify the culprit. If these pranks stop here and now, I will end my investigation and we'll all go on with business as usual." He let out a sigh. "But if they continue, I will find out who you are on my own, or do so with the help of the authorities. This is your one and only warning. Thank you for your attention, everyone."

When the announcement was over, the class was buzzing with this latest news.

"Damaged school property?" Sam asked. "Which prank was that?"

Noah pointed to his blue face. "Hello?"

"Dude, you're not school property," I told him.

"You guys didn't hear about the water fountains?" Jamal Watts asked.

The three of us shook our heads.

Jamal pulled out his phone. "I saw the whole thing." He swiped across his screen until a video came up. We gathered around his phone as a shaky image of two girls at a water fountain appeared—Ashley

Robbins and Deena Bittick. They backed away from the two fountains as something white poured from one of the basins and onto the floor. Deena's face was dripping wet, and the speaker blared out other students laughing.

"What is that?" Noah asked, pointing to the oozing white material.

"It's snow," Jamal replied with a grin. "Well, fake snow."

"I remember that stuff," Sam said. "Mrs. Gaines showed it to us last year."

She was right. Our usual chemistry teacher showed us this highly absorbent polymer powder that expands to nearly one hundred times its original volume when you add water. The end result is pretty realistic.

"Someone must've put a bunch of that powder down the drains," Jamal surmised.

Sam scratched her head. "Why is Deena's face wet?"

"I don't know," Jamal replied. "I only caught the end of the prank."

Noah laughed. "Yeah, I bought some of that fake snow one time. Pretty cool."

I shot him a look. "Oh, so the pranks are funny again, are they?"

Noah's smile faded as he touched the side of his blue face. "No."

After Jamal returned to his work group, Sam gave us a knowing look. "So that had to be what Mr. Davenport meant about damaging school property."

"Yeah, that stuff probably clogged the pipes," I agreed. "They may have to get a plumber in to replace them."

"Or Mr. Jacobs will have to . . ." Noah trailed off as Andrew walked over.

"Hey, Junior," he said. "Did you or your . . . *friends*"— he shot Sam a look—"tell Davenport that I did all the pranks?"

Sam assumed a wide-eyed innocent expression. "Why would we ever do that?"

"Yeah, it's not like you have a history sabotaging this school or anything," Noah added.

"No," I replied. "None of us said a thing to Mr. Davenport."

"Well, I spent all of last period in his office telling him I didn't do it." Andrew glanced around. "Hardly anyone is talking to me anymore. And the ones who do just keep telling me how cool all the pranks are."

Sam crossed her arms. "Well, if the shoe fits."

"Yeah," Noah agreed. "You hacked our robot, so hacking the school security cameras must've been a piece of cake."

I forgot that I hadn't told my friends that the security cameras were no longer an issue. I opened my mouth to explain, but changed my mind. It was too good watching Andrew squirm.

He sighed, then pulled up a stool to our table. As he sat, he glanced around, then leaned forward. The three of us scooted closer. It looked like it was confession time.

"Look," Andrew began. "All right. I hacked your dumb robot." He nodded at Noah. "It was an *actual* piece of cake, by the way. You should really update your firewall, Papa Smurf."

Noah bit his lower lip and shook his head. "Man . . ."

The slam on Noah went completely over my head. I think I was too shocked that Andrew Foger had actually admitted to doing something wrong.

He glanced over at Sam. "And I'm sorry you got blamed for all that stuff at camp. I heard the rumor, saw an opportunity, and ran with it."

Sam sat silently, tight-lipped. I could tell she was fuming.

Andrew's usual smirk disappeared as his gaze moved

over each of us. "I did not hack into the school's security system, though, and I didn't pull all those pranks."

Sam shook her head. "Whatever."

Andrew looked between Noah and me, waiting for a response. After a few seconds of our silence, he pushed off the table and stood. "Fine. Believe what you want," he snapped before spinning around and marching back to his worktable.

"Piece of cake? Really?" Noah asked. "I *know* my program is more secure than the school's system."

Sam raised an eyebrow. "And how do you know that?"

Noah shrugged. "I just know. All right?"

"Yeah, about those security cameras . . . ," I said before explaining what I'd discovered.

"You're just telling us this now?" Sam asked.

Noah crossed his arms. "More importantly, you didn't take me camera-hunting with you."

"I didn't have a chance until now," I told Sam. "And I was just acting on a hunch," I explained to Noah.

He rubbed his blue chin. "So good ol' Andy planted his own digital cameras, then pulled them later when no one was looking. He must've mounted them with that reusable putty or something."

"Then he took the camera footage and edited it together with all the uploaded phone videos," Sam added.

That gave me an idea. I went over to Jamal's table. "Can you pull up that video again, and can I borrow your phone for a second?"

"Sure," Jamal said as he fished out his phone.

After he cued up the video, I brought the phone back to our table. "Let me see something."

Sam and Noah crowded in as I played the shaky video again. As Ashley and Deena reacted to the unexpected blizzard, I scanned the wall behind the fountain. I paused the video when I spotted what I'd been looking for.

"There," I said, pointing to a tiny square on the wall. "I bet that's one of the cameras."

"Oh, yeah," Noah said, taking the phone from me. He played the video again, and then paused it on another frame. The camera wasn't as blurry in that frame.

"I recognize that kind of camera," Sam said. "It's the ones snowboarders wear on their helmets."

She was right. Skydivers, surfers, and all kinds of other athletes use the small digital cameras to get awesome footage of their stunts.

"Man, those things are expensive," Noah said. "But you said Andrew's dad is crazy rich, right?"

"Yeah," I agreed. "If Andrew did it, then buying these cameras wouldn't be a problem."

"If? *If* he did it?" Sam demanded. "Don't tell me you fell for that line he just gave us?"

I hated to admit it, but I actually kind of had.

10

The Inaudible Assertion

THAT NIGHT, I FINISHED MY HOMEWORK AS quickly as I could, and then pulled up the *Not-So-Swift Academy* blog. Sure enough, footage of more pranks had been uploaded. I opened a video called "Let It Snow."

As before, the blurred blogger sat in front of a moving background. This time, thick snowflakes fell from above.

"It's never too early for a little wintry fun, right?" the blogger said in the same deep, distorted voice. "Let's see how a couple of not-so-swift students deal with malfunctioning drinking fountains."

The video cut to an overhead view of the two side-by-side fountains. No doubt, the scene was recorded from the camera we'd spotted in Jamal's video.

Nothing happened at first; students walked past the fountains on their way to class. Then Ashley and Deena came into view. Ashley began drinking from one fountain while Deena moved to the other. She leaned in and pressed the button, but instead of the usual small arc of water flowing from the nozzle, a thin stream shot straight up, blasting her face. She sputtered, stumbling back. I could make out a few strains of laughter in the background.

Meanwhile, Ashley was oblivious to what had just happened to her friend. She kept drinking until the fake snow pushed out of the drain. Suddenly, she stepped back as the basin quickly filled and began overflowing onto the floor. More laughter echoed through the hallway, and there was even some applause.

I couldn't resist chuckling, but stopped abruptly when I realized how embarrassed Deena had been.

The camera angle cut several times, switching to video that must have been shot on a phone. No doubt, the blogger had grabbed footage from other students' uploaded videos.

I rewound the video and concentrated on the camera angles instead of the action. I counted three hidden cameras. Two must have been mounted on the drinking fountain wall—one on each side to get the best shot of both drinkers. It looked like a third camera had been mounted on the wall directly opposite the fountains—this one caught a wide shot of all the action.

Next, I played a video called "False Alarm," which began with an air horn floating behind the blogger.

"These not-so-swift students can't even follow simple instructions," the blogger stated. "See what happens when one of them meets a button that's clearly labeled 'Do not push.'"

The video cut to another hallway scene. I watched Noah walk past the button, come back and examine it, then glance around the hall before finally pressing it. I shook my head as he jumped back in surprise.

In the first minute of the video, I counted three static camera angles just as before. Yet, after Noah pressed the button (then frantically pressed it over and over again to make the alarm shut off), the video began intercutting with phone footage as more students gathered. I even saw Amy and me enter frame with our hands over our ears, shouting to Noah over the noise. Near the end of the video, as Noah pried open the box, the scene cut between the two static cameras on the wall just as my friend got a face full of blue liquid.

As I navigated back to the blogger's main page, I wondered if Noah had gotten any tips from Mr. Osborne on how to get the blue stain off his face. My thoughts were interrupted, however, when I saw that a new clip had been uploaded. It was called "Happy Birthday."

The footage opened with the blurred blogger seated in the same position as in the other videos. This time, a cartoon birthday cake floated in the background.

"It's called the Not-So-Swift Academy for a reason," the blogger said. "Even the faculty is clueless. Let's peek in on a school meeting, shall we?"

The scene cut to an overhead view of our library. All of the Swift Academy's teachers were sitting at tables facing the front, Mr. Davenport leaning against the librarian's desk addressing them. I inched forward, holding my breath. How was the blogger going to prank the teachers?

"The last order of business, of course, is the rash of school pranks," Mr. Davenport said. "Does anyone have any clue as to which student is responsible?"

For a moment, the room remained silent. I felt a little guilty spying on my teachers, especially if they were about to begin theorizing as to who the prankster was. I wasn't sure I was prepared to hear their opinions of different students.

"Have you looked into—" Mr. Varma began before being cut off by high-pitched music. I recognized the tune right away. It was "Happy Birthday."

Mr. Davenport glanced around. "What is that?"

Mrs. Welch stood and moved toward one of the bookshelves. The camera angle shifted so she was in the foreground. The librarian sorted through some books until she pulled out a small object. The music grew louder as she carried it over to the principal.

"What is this from, a birthday card?" he asked, turning it over in his hands.

I nodded as I recognized the object. After all, what curious kid hadn't examined the mechanisms behind a singing greeting card, poking at the tiny speaker and battery attached to an even smaller circuit board?

Mr. Davenport pinched the circuit board until his fingers came away with a silver disc. He must've removed the battery, since the music cut off mid-verse. He held up the device. "See? This is what I'm—"

He was interrupted by another round of "Happy Birthday."

There were a few chuckles as the teachers' heads turned in the opposite direction to where the first device had been found. This time, Mr. Edge quickly located the musical culprit. He didn't bother handing it to the principal, popping out the battery himself.

No sooner had that device been silenced than another one went off. Then another. And another. After what seemed like a dozen more digital trills, the usually quiet library was suddenly awash with birthday songs playing out of sync. The cacophony sounded maddening to me. I could only imagine what it was like to actually be there, in the middle of a "Happy Birthday" insane surround sound. All the teachers were searching for the offending devices. After about a minute of the irritating scavenger hunt, the video cut off.

I leaned back in my chair. No wonder Mr. Davenport had decided to crack down on the pranks. I bet he was furious after being a target himself.

I thought back to what Sam had said about Andrew. Sure, if he was the blogger, of course he would deny it. But honestly, I didn't think he was that good a liar. I was no Andrew Foger fan by a long shot, but he had seemed sincere.

I had an idea. Maybe if I watched the videos again with a different ear, I could pick out a speech pattern or common phrase that Andrew used. The blogger was using some kind of voice distortion, but I didn't think Andrew was clever enough to change the rhythm of his speech pattern or to scrub habitual expressions from his vocabulary. I almost wished the blogger had said, "That's for me to know and you to find out." Then I'd know for certain.

Since "Happy Birthday" was already open, I began there. I restarted the video and listened carefully, purposely not looking at the blurred face and trying to imagine, instead, Andrew saying those words. Had I ever heard him use the word "faculty" before?

Just before the video cut to the library, movement in the corner of the screen caught my eye. I hit pause and backed the time bar up a bit, then leaned closer to my monitor as the footage played again. *There!* A triangle appeared in the top right corner of the screen. I played the segment back again and figured out what it was that was bothering me. The top right corner of the blogger's green screen had fallen, revealing part of the background behind it. Was that a tree? It was difficult to make out.

I had to get more eyes on this.

I shot a group text to my friends, and within moments, their faces appeared on my computer screen in a video chat.

"What's up, Swift?" Sam asked.

"Did you guys watch the latest video on *Not-So-Swift*?" I asked.

Noah cracked up. "Oh, yeah. No wonder Davenport has it in for the prankster."

"At least it didn't destroy school property this time," Amy chimed in.

"Okay, I found something weird in the intro to that video." I explained how the backdrop appeared to fall down. "Check it out. It's about at forty-five seconds in."

I waited while each of my friends pulled up the video.

"Hey, what is that?" Noah asked.

"I don't know," I replied. "It looks like a tree or something."

"It *is* a tree," Sam confirmed. She turned and pointed to her back wall. "I have the same eco poster on my wall. Can you see it?"

I leaned closer to the monitor. The poster was tiny in the corner of Sam's chat screen, but I could just make out the tree in the background. It was the same thing.

Noah shrugged. "So the blogger has the same poster. So what?"

Amy leaned in closer as she examined the image. "Not just the same poster. Literally the same poster."

Sam cocked her head. "What are you talking about?"

"It's in the exact same position as in one of your videos," Amy explained. "The one about your thumbprint key card."

Sam had invented a cool access card that read fingerprints the way some phones do. She had showed if off at school and later made a video explaining how it worked.

"How do you know that?" Noah asked.

"Dude, photographic memory, remember?" I told him. "Amy's superpower."

She really did have it and it was spooky sometimes, let me tell you.

Amy typed something on her keyboard. "Let me get my editing software up and running and I'll show you."

Within moments, Amy sent me a video. I assumed she'd sent the same one to Sam and Noah.

I opened the clip to see Sam explaining her key card. There was no sound, but there didn't need to be—sure enough, the tree poster was there in the upper right corner, in the same exact place. To prove her point even more, Amy had edited in a few seconds of the blogger's video. The entire scene changed except for the poster. It was a perfect match.

Noah's eyes went wide. "You're the blurred blogger, Sam?"

"Of course not," she replied. "But someone wants people to think I am. Sound familiar, Swift?"

It did. It was just like what Andrew did at camp.

"This seems like a stretch," I told her. "How many people are going to notice that?"

"You did," Sam shot back.

"Yeah, but who else will know it's your poster?"

"I did," Amy replied.

"Yeah, Amy," Noah said. "But you're . . . Amy."

Sam shook her head. "In a school like ours, all it'll take is a couple of people figuring it out. After that, the rumors will start all over again."

I sunk lower in my chair. She was right. The students at the academy lived for stuff like this. Not the spreading-rumors part—that was just a teenager thing. But now that Sam mentioned it, I bet students had been analyzing these videos for days, trying to figure out who was behind the pranks.

"I can't believe it," Sam said. "Andrew Foger is pinning the blame on me again."

11

The Impending Impediment

WHEN I ARRIVED AT SCHOOL THE NEXT DAY, I quickly realized how right Sam was. I hadn't even made it to my locker before Terry Stephenson asked me if I had known Sam was the prankster. From there, I got similar questions from Barry Jacobs and Collin Webb.

When I reached algebra, Noah and Amy were already there. Sam's desk was empty.

Noah shook his head as I slid into my desk. "Sam totally called it." His face still had a bit of a blue tint to it, but I was too wrapped up in the rumors to give him grief.

"It's crazy," I said, and then told him about my three encounters.

"From what I've heard so far, the school is split," Noah explained. "Half think Andrew is the prankster, trying to frame Sam. The other half just think Sam's doing it all."

"There's another camp," Amy added. "I heard a theory that Sam was the prankster all along, but it's part of a big plan to get back at Andrew for what he did at the summer camp."

Noah nodded thoughtfully. "That's a good one."

"But that doesn't make sense," I said. "The first prank happened before Sam even knew Andrew was here."

Amy shrugged. "That's just what I heard."

"Too bad it isn't true." Noah grinned. "That would be the perfect payback."

I motioned to Sam's empty desk. "Where is she?"

Amy shook her head. "I don't know."

"Oh, man, I hope she didn't skip," Noah said. "That totally makes her look guilty."

As the rest of the class filed in, Sam still didn't show up. Even Andrew made it just before the bell rang. He caught me glancing from Sam's empty desk to his in the back and glared at me. "What?" he mouthed.

I spun back around as class began. As Mr. Jenkins started explaining the lesson, I thought of what Andrew had said the day before. He'd seemed so convincing when he proclaimed his innocence. This thing with Sam was right out of his playbook, but maybe that's what someone wanted everyone to think. Most everyone in the school knew about what went down at the camp. And if they didn't know already, they had to have heard it by now. Could Andrew be getting a taste of his own medicine? Was someone capitalizing on a rumor about him?

I tried to put the theory out of my mind and focus on Mr. Jenkins's lecture. Of course, it wasn't easy to keep that focus when Sam finally entered the classroom a few minutes later.

"Good of you to join us, Miss Watson," Mr. Jenkins said, an eyebrow raised.

"Sorry," Sam mumbled as she walked to the front of the classroom and handed him her tardy slip.

Mr. Jenkins glanced at the paper before tossing it on his desk. "Now, where were we?" He returned to writing out formulas on the electronic board.

Noah and I both spun around as Sam slid into her desk.

"I thought you were skipping for sure," Noah whispered.

Sam rolled her eyes as she pulled her tablet and notebook from her backpack. "I was in Davenport's office."

Amy covered her mouth. "You're in trouble already?"

Sam leaned in, keeping her voice low. "No, I decided to get ahead of this rumor and tell him about it myself."

I raised an eyebrow. "That's brave," I whispered. "What did he say?"

"No one had told him about the rumor yet," she replied. "And he doesn't think I'm the prankster. . . . I think?"

"You think?" Noah demanded.

Sam shook her head. "I got the feeling that he's not ruling anyone out."

I edged forward. "But you coming to him in the first place—"

"You getting all this, Mr. Swift?" Mr. Jenkins asked, his arms crossed.

Noah and I spun back around, and I began madly copying the formulas from the board. "Yes, sir. Sorry."

A chuckle rippled through the class. Andrew's laugh lingered a little longer than everyone else's, and I shook my head, annoyed at him all over again.

We didn't get anything else out of Sam for the rest of class, or right after, for that matter. I guess we'd have to wait for lunch to get all the juicy details about her meeting with the principal.

The rest of the morning was pretty standard. I refuted occasional rumors whenever someone asked about Sam being the prankster. I found it odd that no one asked me if I thought Andrew was responsible, though. Either the students who believed that rumor didn't need my confirmation, or they simply assumed I believed the story too.

I caught myself keeping an eye out for hidden cameras. Maybe I was worrying about nothing. For all I knew, the blurred blogger would take Mr. Davenport's advice and stop pulling stunts. But then why had they posted the "Happy Birthday" video? Of course, why waste the chance to show it to the world and get a last dig at all the teachers? I wasn't sure why, but I had a feeling that it wouldn't be the last prank by a long shot.

When I got to chemistry I slid onto my stool next to Amy. "Did Sam say anything else about her meeting with Davenport?"

Amy shook her head. "We didn't get a chance to talk yet."

"All right, gang," Mr. Osborne said as he closed the door and moved back to his desk, putting his hand on a large silver canister. "We're going to keep the cool theme going this week with some liquid nitrogen."

I leaned forward. Liquid nitrogen was way cool—literally. It's used in freezing food, cooling super-conductors, and cryogenics. Liquid nitrogen was like dry ice on steroids. I didn't want to tell Mr. Osborne that Mrs. Gaines had already given us a cool demo of the stuff earlier this year, flash-freezing roses and then shattering them on a hard surface. I wondered what he was planning.

I was so interested in the upcoming lesson that it took me a moment to realize someone had been nudging my shoulder. When the nudge became a hard poke, it clicked that Amy was trying to get my attention. Her eyes were wide, scared behind her safety glasses.

"What is it?" I asked quietly.

She pointed past me, and then quickly shielded her face with her long hair.

I turned and scanned the class. I didn't see anyone doing anything that would justify that reaction. And then I realized that she hadn't been pointing at our fellow students, but at something beyond them. As soon I spotted it, I felt a bowling ball in my stomach. High on the wall, pointing down at us, was one of the hidden cameras.

Something big was about to go down.

12

The Chemistry Confinement

I COULDN'T BELIEVE IT. HERE I WAS, THINKING I was paranoid looking for cameras all day, then I drop my guard for just a moment and walk right into ground zero. After a quick glance around the room, I counted three cameras in total. Two were mounted on the wall by the door and one was mounted on the opposite side above the windows. The two on my left were trained on the students. The one on my right was aimed straight at Mr. Osborne.

I quickly slid on my safety glasses as Amy had done. Was the prank going to have something to do with liquid nitrogen? I hoped not. Like dry ice, that stuff could give someone a nasty case of frostbite if it splashed onto their skin.

I leaned closer to Amy. "Should we tell somebody?"

"I don't know," she whispered, keeping her head down, her face curtained off from the cameras.

I glanced over at Andrew's worktable. He wasn't acting suspicious, like he knew something was about to happen. If he truly *was* the blogger, maybe this prank wouldn't be so bad. After all, why would he want to harm or humiliate himself? However, if he or someone else in the lab was the prankster, would me saying something actually do anything? They might simply call it off or not go through with it. Either way, it felt silly interrupting Mr. Osborne just because I'd noticed a few cameras. After another moment, I decided to wait and see what would happen.

I'm sure Mr. Osborne's demonstration was very interesting, but I have to admit that I wasn't paying close attention. My eyes kept darting to the three cameras, trying to pinpoint exactly what they'd record. When I wasn't studying the cameras, I was glancing around the room trying to spot anyone acting strangely. Was a cabinet full of snakes going to fly open or something? Then again, this *was* the chemistry lab, so I couldn't rule out that something might blow up. The bowling ball in my stomach now felt like a twisting knot.

I glanced over at Amy and could tell she was feeling the tension too. Even with her hair curtaining her face, I saw her eyes darting around like mine, and she was panting a little. Whatever was going to happen, I hoped it started soon, or I worried that she'd have a panic attack.

"At normal pressure, liquid nitrogen boils at minus one hundred and ninety-eight degrees Celsius," Mr. Osborne explained. "Nitrogen was first liquefied back in 1883 by Polish physicists Karol Olszewski and Zygmunt . . ." His voice croaked on the second name, and he cleared his throat and tried again. "Zygmunt . . ." Mr. Osborne's voice was considerably lower in pitch that time. He cleared his throat again. "I don't know what's . . ." His voice was even lower.

My fellow students lost it, but instead of sounding like a bunch of twelve- and thirteen-year-olds laughing, the room echoed with the deep rumbles of adult voices.

I turned to Amy. "Is this the prank?" I asked in a deep baritone.

Amy's eyes went wide as her "Wow" came out an octave lower than normal.

The classroom was soon filled with low-voiced chatter. I even heard a couple renditions of "Luke, I am your father."

"Hang on. I think I know what happened," Mr. Osborne said before disappearing into the supply room.

The class broke out in deep guffawing again.

A few seconds later, Mr. Osborne returned holding a large gas tank, twisting the valve shut as he made his way back to the front of the room. "Someone opened the tank of sulfur hexafluoride. I was saving this for next week, but I guess we're getting a crash course now." He set the tank down on his desk. "Sulfur hexafluoride is six times heavier than air. You know how breathing helium makes your voice higher? Well, this stuff turns your vocal cords into a subwoofer."

Everything he said was fascinating, but it was hard to take him seriously when his voice sounded like that.

Maggie Ortiz raised her hand. "Is it safe to breathe?" Since her voice was so deep, her question was met with another surge of laughter.

Mr. Osborne waved her away. "Some people report

irritation to their lungs and throat, but it's nontoxic." He pointed to the other side of the room. "Let's get those windows open and air out the place."

I leapt off my stool and moved to the nearest window. Two other students followed my lead. But when I flipped the latch and pushed out, the pane didn't budge. I pushed harder. Still nothing. I saw that the others weren't having any better luck.

"They won't open," I said in my new strange baritone.

"What?" Kyle Swan asked, a twinge of panic in his booming voice. Nervous chatter rippled through the room.

"All right, settle down," Mr. Osborne ordered. "Let's go out into the hall."

Kyle got to the door first and swung it open, moving to step across the threshold, but halted abruptly. More accurately, he was stopped by the thick plastic film stretched across the entryway. He came up short so suddenly that other students slammed into his back, piling up behind him. The clear film stretched from the load, but didn't break.

Now everyone really was panicking. Even Andrew seemed worried, his eyes darting around, looking for the next attack.

"Hang on," Mr. Osborne said as he pulled some scissors from his desk drawer. He peeled students away from the pileup, pushing his way to the door, before poking through the plastic and cutting a long slit down the center. Once he'd yanked, creating a wide enough gap, we began climbing through. In no time at all, the entire chemistry class was milling around in the hallway. Now that everyone was away from the gas, our voices quickly went back to normal.

"Nice going," Kyle said, glaring at Andrew. Other students joined in the furious grumbling.

Andrew raised both hands. "Don't look at me! I don't even know what sulfur flexa-whatever is."

I studied Andrew's face. He seemed sincere and a little embarrassed by all the negative attention. I didn't know what to think.

Amy nudged me and pointed to the wall opposite the chemistry lab door. I knew what she'd seen before I even looked up.

Sure enough, a fourth camera was mounted there, perfectly positioned to capture our escape from the lab.

13

The Appropriation Operation

"NO WAY," NOAH SAID BETWEEN BITES OF HIS sandwich. "I saw a demo of that stuff online. How did it feel, talking like that?"

"Really weird," I replied. "But the worst part was thinking we were trapped in the lab."

Sam stabbed at her salad. "I bet Andrew was gloating the entire time."

I shook my head. "He seemed kind of freaked out too."

"All part of the act," she said before taking a bite.

"It seems weird that he would prank himself, doesn't it?" I asked.

"Dude, it's the *perfect* thing to do," Noah countered. "Take some of the suspicion off."

"I guess so." I poked at my lunch with my spork. If only my friends had seen the fear in Andrew's eyes. I still didn't think he was that good an actor.

Amy shook her head. "The worst part was noticing the cameras, waiting for something to happen."

"I'm surprised you didn't have a panic attack," Sam told her.

"I almost did," Amy confessed. "It was very stressful."

"Did either of you tell Mr. Osborne about the cameras?" Sam asked. "Those things probably have memory cards that store the video. If he were to confiscate them, then neither of you would end up in the latest addition to the *Not-So-Swift* blog."

"I didn't even think about the memory cards," I admitted.

"Wait a minute." Noah slammed down his spork and grinned. "I just had a brilliant idea."

"What?" I asked.

"Quick, did any of those cameras have an antenna of some kind?"

"Uh, I didn't really—"

Noah waved me off. "Not you. Amy, what do you think?"

She looked up and to the left. We all knew that was her way of accessing her photographic memory. She looks up and to the right when she's looking at her near-perfect internal clock. The girl really had some spooky superpowers.

"No, there weren't any," she reported.

Noah clapped his hands and grinned. After a moment, he blurted out, "Don't you get it?"

We exchanged glances. I don't think any of us had a clue what he was talking about.

"You'll have to give us more than that," Sam finally said.

Noah leaned back in his chair. "Oh, man. I don't know why I didn't think of this sooner."

"What?" I demanded.

He leaned forward and pushed his tray aside. "Okay, if the cameras had antennae, then they probably transmitted the video somewhere else. There would be no reason to have a memory card."

"Yeah? And?" Sam asked.

"So no antennae means that they *do* have memory cards," Noah said proudly.

Sam threw up her hands. "That's what I said two minutes ago."

Noah pointed a finger at her. "Yeah, but no antennae also means they can't be remotely triggered."

"Okay . . . so . . ." I still didn't see why he was so excited.

"So?" Noah's eyes gleamed. "*So* that means the cameras have to be switched on manually. Don't you get it?"

Amy's hands shot up to her mouth. "That means the prankster is on video when he turns on the camera."

Noah pointed at Amy with both hands. "And there it is!"

Amy was as excited as Noah now. "All he would have to do is edit himself out of the footage before cutting the final video together."

Noah shook his head. "I don't know why I didn't think of it before. All we need to do is get one of the cameras and read the memory card, and we'll have iron-clad proof of who the prankster is."

I shot to my feet. "I have to get one of those cameras."

"I'll come with," Noah said as he grabbed his tray.

Sam stood and peered around the cafeteria. "Wait a minute. Where's Andrew?"

The rest of us followed her gaze. I didn't spot him anywhere.

"Well, if you see him, stall him," Noah instructed.

"Stall him?" Sam asked. "How?"

Noah shrugged. "I don't know. Scare him some more about how you're going to get him back for framing you."

Sam smiled. "Oh, yeah. That's been fun."

Noah and I dumped our trays and headed for the door at a brisk pace, trying not to look too conspicuous. Once we'd made it through the doorway, we broke into a run. Luckily, the chemistry lab was just a couple doors away. Not so luckily, as we got closer, I could already see that the camera in the hallway had vanished.

I pointed up at the spot where it had been earlier. "That one's gone already."

"Aw, man," Noah said. "But maybe that was just the easiest one to grab."

I led the way, pushing open the classroom door. My eyes immediately scanned the wall above the windows. That camera was gone too.

"Can I help you gentlemen?" someone asked.

Noah and I both jumped, startled to see that Mr.

Osborne was sitting as his desk. He had a lunch tray on his left and a stack of papers on his right.

Noah put a hand on my shoulder. "Tom here lost his favorite pen. Maybe he left it in here?"

"Uh, yeah" was all I could get out.

"He's always talking about it," Noah continued.

Mr. Osborne gave a dismissive wave as he returned his attention to the stack of papers. "Sure. Go ahead and have a look."

Noah followed me as I moved to my worktable, both of us crouching down, making a big show of searching for this imaginary pen. As I pretended to scan the floor, I glanced up at the opposite wall. My shoulders dropped when I saw that the two cameras that had been there earlier were nowhere in sight. I nudged Noah and nodded up at the wall. He shook his head, disappointed.

Noah stood. "You must've left it in the computer lab."

"Uh, right. That's probably it," I agreed, trying to sound convincing. We headed for the door. "Thanks, Mr. Osborne."

"No problem," he said. "With all the excitement in class today, you weren't the only student to run off and leave things behind."

"Oh, yeah?" I asked. "Someone else lost something?"

Mr. Osborne didn't look up from the papers. "Yes," he replied. "Andrew Foger was in here when I got back with my lunch."

14

The Articulation Revelation

"PER YOUR PRINCIPAL'S REQUEST, I'VE HAD some of my people look into this blogger's identity and his website," my dad said as he loaded the dishwasher. "Trouble is, his videos seem to upload from different servers all over the world. Very slick masking setup."

I rinsed off the last dish. "Is that something a student could pull off?" Even though Andrew had hacked our robot, I didn't know if he had the skills to mask his server.

"Oh, sure," my dad replied. "Even if someone doesn't have the know-how, there's plenty of software out there that can help."

Andrew did have the funds to buy his way into being a master hacker, that was for sure.

"This latest prank might give us a legal in," my dad explained. I had already told him about what had happened in chemistry class. "Even though sulfur hexafluoride is an inert gas, trapping a bunch of students in a classroom just might get a judge to agree to signing an injunction. I have some of my legal team working on that too."

"Cool," I said as I dried my hands.

It felt good having my dad's people working on uncovering the prankster. I hadn't told him about Noah's and my failed attempt to get one of the cameras and unmask the blogger that way. It had seemed like a good idea at the time, but it had only ended up making Andrew look guiltier. And it had been my dad who gave me the big speech about second chances and everything.

"How are things going with Andrew?" he asked, as if reading my mind.

I jumped. "What? Oh, okay, I guess."

My father raised an eyebrow. "Mr. Davenport told me about the rumors going around that Andrew is the prankster."

I sighed. "Yeah, I had heard that too." I left out that

my friends believed the rumor and that I was shifting toward their view of things again.

My dad leaned against the counter. "What do you think?"

I nervously rubbed the back of my neck. "I don't know. It's kind of his style and everything."

"Did you ask him about it?"

I nodded. "Yeah. He denied it."

My father shrugged. "Well, there you go. Maybe he's telling the truth."

"I guess so."

I thought about mentioning all the evidence against Andrew over the past few days: his hacking of Raider, trying to frame Sam, him showing up in chemistry during lunch. But with my dad putting in a good word for Andrew in the first place, I didn't want to accuse him unless we had absolute proof. The trouble was, how would we get it?

When Dad and I were finished in the kitchen, I went upstairs to my bedroom and dug into my homework. I had a particularly heavy load that night and it felt good to get my mind off the pranks for a while. That lasted for a good hour, but just as I was finishing up, it was my turn to be invited to a four-way video chat. I accepted the request and my screen was once again filled with the faces of my three friends.

"Dude, did you see the new video?" Noah asked.

I shook my head. "I've been taking a break from the whole thing. Is it the chemistry gas attack?"

"Just watch it, Swift," Sam said through tight lips. "We'll wait."

I minimized the chat screens and pulled up the blogger's website. A new video entitled "The Dark Side" was at the top of the list.

The scene opened the same as usual: The blogger sat in front of another animated background, except this time, a cartoon image of Darth Vader's helmet floated behind him. I noted that the poster corner at the top right of the screen had been put back up.

"All right, gang," the blogger began in the same creepy voice. "Check out what happens when an entire classroom full of the not-so-swift students goes through puberty all at once."

I shook my head as the scene changed to the interior of the classroom. The camera angle shifted among all three cameras as everyone's voices deepened. Then, as everyone panicked and raced for the door, the video cut to the hallway as a bunch of students shoved against the plastic covering the doorway. If I hadn't been there, it might've been funny seeing Kyle Swan's nose pressed to one side as his face pushed against the transparent barrier.

I minimized the web page and brought my friends' faces to the foreground. "Okay, I saw the video. I was there, remember?"

Noah laughed. "I told you he wouldn't see it."

"See what?" I asked.

"It's very hard to catch," Amy admitted.

"Catch what?"

"Ah, come on." Noah pointed at his screen. "I spotted it right away."

Sam was silent, just shaking her head.

"Come on, guys," I pleaded. "What am I missing?"

Noah leaned closer. "Okay, go back to the beginning. It's right around where the blogger says 'classroom.'"

I kept my friends' windows open as I rewound the video near the beginning.

". . . check out what happens when an entire classroom full of the not-so-swift students—"

I paused the video. Just as Noah had predicted, near

the word "classroom," something flashed onto the blogger's face.

"What was that?" I asked.

"You have to go frame by frame," Amy instructed. "It only happens for a single frame, about eight seconds in."

I rewound the clip to six seconds and began advancing the video frame by frame, tapping on my keyboard as the blogger moved in jerky motions. Then, when the timeline hit eight seconds, I saw it: The constant blur that had covered the blogger's face from the very beginning suddenly vanished, and the blogger's real face was revealed.

It was Sam.

I leaned in toward my screen. "What?!"

"He did it again," Sam said.

Noah rolled his eyes. "Can you believe this guy?"

"How?" I asked.

"He must've grabbed a frame from one of Sam's videos," Amy explained. "And then put her face over his."

I had heard of software that could digitally take people's faces, put them in videos, and then have them say anything. But I'm guessing it would be way easier to just drop in a single frame over an existing video.

Sam looked like she was going to pop. "This guy's gone way too far this time."

"It's just a single frame," I said. "Do you think anyone will notice?"

"Dude, *I* noticed," Noah said. "And I wasn't even looking."

Sam leaned closer, looming in her video frame. "We have to take Andrew Foger down."

"My dad is working on it." I shared what my dad had said about his people uncovering the blogger's identity.

Sam shook her head. "Not fast enough, Swift. We need to find one of those cameras tomorrow and get hard evidence."

"The trouble is, if you spot a camera, that means you're next in line for a prank," I explained.

"Tom, you could follow Andrew," Noah suggested. "See if you can catch him in the act. He's in all your classes, so it won't look suspicious."

"What if he's already set up the next one?" Amy asked. "He hangs out after school a lot."

Sam nodded. "Even better. Then we search the school tomorrow for cameras."

I sighed. "All right, I will. But right now, I have to go. I still haven't finished my homework."

"Aw, man. You're not done yet?" Noah asked with a grin before he logged out.

"Bye, Tom," said Amy waving just before her window vanished.

Sam reached for her keyboard. "We're counting on you tomorrow." Her window disappeared too.

I returned my attention to my homework, but it was difficult to concentrate. I felt anxious about trailing Andrew all day tomorrow. I knew it was necessary and it would be great to catch him in the act. I just hoped I could pull it off without getting caught.

A few minutes later, I glanced up at my computer screen and noticed the prank video was still frozen there. I was about to close it, but then stopped. Was there something I'd missed (besides Sam's face, anyway) that would help point to Andrew as the culprit? He'd seemed just as surprised by the chemistry classroom prank as I was. But would the video show something more? I hit play.

The blurred blogger finished the intro and the scene cut to the classroom, as before. Again, Mr. Osborne was the first to have his voice deepen. Then, one by one, students spoke in lower voices. It wasn't long before everyone sounded like the blurred blogger.

I paused the video.

Something nagged at the back of my mind—something about the way we all sounded and how similar it was to the blogger. I'm sure when he made each video, he didn't breathe sulfur hexafluoride to disguise his voice. There were tons of voice modulators out there that did the job digitally. Yet I couldn't help feeling that the detail wasn't just a coincidence.

I restarted the video.

"All right, gang," the blogger began again. "Check out what happens when an entire classroom full of the not-so-swift students—"

I paused the video.

There was something there, staring me in the face, and it wasn't Sam's. Something about the blogger's voice.

I restarted the video.

"All right, gang," the blogger repeated. "Check out what happens when an entire classroom full of—"

I restarted the video.

"All right, gang—"

I restarted the clip again and again.

"All right, gang . . . All right, gang . . . All right, gang . . ."

I stopped the video and leaned back in my chair. I held my breath as a chill went down my spine.

I knew exactly who the blogger was.

15

The Implication Confirmation

"MR. OSBORNE?!"

"Shh!" I glared at Noah, then glanced around our algebra classroom to make sure no one had overheard him.

His mouth fell open and he shook his head. "Mr. Osborne? Really?" This time he whispered, thankfully.

"I'll tell you how I know."

"How you know what?" Sam asked as she and Amy took their seats.

Amy glanced back at Andrew's empty desk. "Do you know where Andrew is right now?"

I shook my head. "No, and it doesn't matter because he's not the prankster."

Sam eyed me suspiciously. "What do you mean?"

Noah crossed his arms. "Oh, you're going to love this."

I glanced around and moved closer to Sam and Amy. They leaned in.

"He thinks it's Mr. Osborne," Noah blurted out. "I'm sorry, man, I couldn't keep that kind of intel in."

"What?" Sam asked.

Amy gave a thoughtful look. "It was his voice, wasn't it? I remember thinking how his altered voice sounded like the blogger's. But then all of our voices sounded like that."

I shook my head. "That's not it. Well . . . that's what made me look closer."

Sam raised an eyebrow. "That's kinda weak, Swift."

"Okay, look . . ." I glanced around again. The class was filling up, but Andrew hadn't arrived yet. "When all this started, I studied the videos, looking for any sign of Andrew's speech patterns. And believe me, he has some annoying ones."

"Oh yeah," Noah agreed.

"Right? But I couldn't find any," I went on. "That's what gave me doubt at first." I grinned. "So I'm rewatching the video from last night and I catch one of Mr. Osborne's speech patterns."

"Which one?" Noah asked.

"You know how every teacher has a different thing they call the class as a group?" I began counting them off on my fingers. "Ladies and gentlemen, boys and girls, just plain 'class'..."

"Mr. Jenkins's 'sports fans,'" Noah added, shaking his head. "For whatever reason."

"Right!" I grinned. "Mr. Osborne always calls us 'gang.' 'Okay, *gang.*' 'Listen up, *gang.*'"

"And that's how the blogger began last night's video," Amy chimed in.

"Exactly!" I said.

Sam shook her head. "That's still weak. One word and he's your prime suspect now?"

"And why would he prank himself?" Noah added.

"You're the one who said the same thing about Andrew," I replied, pointing at my best friend. "How making it appear like he was the target of the prank would take some of the suspicion off himself."

Noah cringed. "Oh, yeah. I did say that, didn't I?"

"Mr. Osborne has access to the gas and chemicals," I explained. "My dad says he's super smart, so he could easily build the rats, and the timers for the sound chips."

"So could most of the kids in this school," Amy pointed out.

Sam shrugged. "I don't know. I say we stick to the original plan. We'll look for cameras. You follow—" She glanced away just as Andrew entered the classroom, then turned back to me. "You know."

"Hey, it's not like you can follow Mr. Osborne around," Noah whispered. "He'll be in his class most of the day anyway."

"All right." I sighed. "I'll follow Andrew as planned."

I could tell there was no convincing my friends. I had laid out all my best evidence, and they still didn't believe me. Maybe it was more difficult believing a teacher was behind the pranks. Then again, it wouldn't be the first time a teacher had been responsible for strange goings-on at the academy.

I decided to follow Andrew, not to catch him in the act but to prove his innocence. If another prank went down today and I could prove Andrew had nothing to do with it, maybe my friends would take a closer look at Mr. Osborne.

I glanced back at Andrew one more time. He was eyeing us suspiciously.

As my friends predicted, following Andrew wasn't all that hard. It helped that he shared all my classes, and that our lockers were near each other. The only difficulty came when he went to the restroom. I hoped he wasn't really the prankster setting up a bathroom prank, because I thought it would be too obvious if I followed him in there. I simply struck up conversations with other students at a place where I could keep an eye on the restroom door.

Once we were in chemistry, I turned my attention to Mr. Osborne. He had to be the prankster; I was sure of it. Unfortunately, he didn't do or say anything during his lecture to give himself away. There were no signs of cameras, and everything went like a normal class.

I reported as much when I met my friends for lunch.

Sam shook her head. "We haven't noticed any cameras either."

"And there haven't been any pranks yet today," Noah added.

"Do you think that last prank was it?" Amy asked.

Sam grinned. "Andrew might be feeling the heat. I've had a bunch of people tell me how sorry they are that he's pinning it on me again."

My friends had been right. Several people were talking about the single frame of Sam's face in the last video. I guess a bunch of the academy students had keener eyes than me. If the clue was meant to point toward Sam, it had backfired. Everyone I talked to seemed convinced Andrew was the prankster now.

Noah rubbed his chin. "And I might've let it slip that Tom's dad had people looking into this whole mess."

"Dude!" I said. My best friend was always terrible at keeping secrets.

"Way to go, Noah," Sam snapped. "How can Tom catch Andrew if he stops pulling pranks?"

Noah shook his head. "No way he's going to stop. Someone like that has to go out with a bang, you know?"

I glanced across the cafeteria. Andrew sat right where I'd seen him last, alone at a table by the wall. I felt sorry for him, and kind of irritated at my friends for not believing me about Mr. Osborne. Sam of all people should know what it's like being blamed for something she didn't do.

"Maybe you're right," Sam admitted to Noah. "Maybe he just hasn't had the chance to set anything up while Tom is following him."

"We could stay after school," Amy suggested. "Maybe he needs the school empty to set up the next prank."

"Excellent idea, Ames," Noah said. "I'm in."

"Me too," Sam agreed.

My three friends looked at me, waiting for my reply.

"Okay." I pulled out my phone. "I'll text my dad." My father never minded staying late to get more work done. That was one of the perks of having his offices right across the street from the academy.

Out of the corner of my eye, I saw Andrew take his tray toward the kitchen. He was on the move.

I sighed and nodded his way. "That's my cue." I took a few more bites before gathering my things.

"Hey, Swift," Sam said. "Maybe you should 'lose' him just after school's out."

"Good idea," Noah said with a grin. "Give him a chance to set up and us a chance to catch him in the act."

"Whatever you say," I said as I picked up my tray.

I lingered a bit longer until Andrew was headed toward the exit, then I quickly dumped my tray. I had no intention of losing him. I wanted to be his alibi when the real prankster made his move.

I followed Andrew from the cafeteria to the computer lab. There were a few other students there, so I was able to sit at a station near the back of the classroom without being noticed. Andrew worked on a computer of his own for the remainder of lunch period.

After that, it was back to business as usual. I trailed him to every class, trying not to be noticed. It would've been easier if Andrew stopped to talk to any of his new friends, like I had seen him do days before. But, instead, Andrew kept to himself, not interacting with anyone. The prankster rumor really seemed to be hitting him hard.

Normally, once I got to robotics class, I'd be able to catch up with my friends—at least Sam and Noah. But today, Mrs. Scott kept everyone busy as she laid out our new assignment. Our groups were to design and build a robot that could ascend and descend stairs. From the gleam in Noah's eyes, I could tell that he was ready to outfit Raider with the new technology once we designed it. I actually agreed. It would be cool to be able to skip the elevator with him once in a while.

After the final bell rang, I followed Andrew to his locker, as I had done all day. And then . . . I lost him. I mean, for real lost him. I had been busy with my own locker, and when I looked back up, he was gone. He must've blended in with the students leaving for the day. I pushed through the crowd, trying to find him again, but it was no good.

Hitching up my backpack, I headed to the gym where my friends and I had planned to meet. As I walked in, I spotted them sitting in the bleachers. Raider patrolled the area in front of them.

"Did you see him do anything?" Sam asked before I had made it halfway across the gym.

I glanced around nervously. We were mostly alone; only two fencers sparred at the other end.

I shook my head. "Not a thing."

Sam clasped her hands together. "Okay, we just wait for the school to clear out some more, and then we catch Andrew in the act."

"Or whoever it is," I added.

Noah put his hands on his hips. "You're still on that?"

I shrugged. "I'm just saying, Andrew didn't do anything suspicious all day." I nodded toward the gym exit.

"Meanwhile, Mr. Osborne could've been setting up his next big prank."

"He has a point," Amy said. "That's why I swung by the chemistry lab every chance I got today."

"Really?" I asked.

Amy shrugged. "But Mr. Osborne was there almost every time I looked in. Sorry, Tom."

Noah pointed at her. "There, you see?"

"I guess so" is what I said. But, no, I didn't see. I just knew I was right about Mr. Osborne.

We killed about thirty minutes waiting for the school to clear. Amy did homework while Sam, Noah, and I put Raider through some exercises. Noah had programmed basic commands and it almost felt as if we were training a real dog.

Sam checked her watch. "Think it's about time?"

We knew the school wouldn't be completely cleared. Many students stayed late to work on projects. But the place should have been deserted enough to let the prankster set up his next trick.

"I think so," I replied. "How about you and Amy take this floor, I'll take the second floor, and Noah takes the third?"

Noah pointed at Raider. "Hard to sneak in and out of an elevator."

Sam rolled her eyes. "Fine. Amy and I will take the third floor."

Amy packed up her stuff, leaving her backpack with ours piled on the bleachers.

"Remember, search every classroom," Noah reminded us. "You never know where he might strike." Raider followed him obediently as we headed for the gym door.

"Got it," I said. But I planned to begin my search in one particular classroom: the chemistry lab—the main reason I'd chosen the floor assignment. I would either trail Mr. Osborne from there or find his stash of supplies.

Sam, Amy, and I hit the stairs. They continued up to the third floor as I got off on the second. I didn't bother searching any of the classrooms along the way, running straight for the chem lab. It was at the opposite end of the school, so I poured on the speed. My eyes locked on the entrance.

When I was about halfway there, the lab door flew open. My heart skipped a beat as I dove into the first alcove I came to. I turned back and peeked around the corner. Someone was exiting the lab carrying one of the stools.

Andrew Foger.

He glanced around before hauling the stool to the wall opposite the door, then climbed on top and stood, reaching toward something mounted on the wall. He seemed to adjust the object before climbing back down. Once back on the ground, he picked up the stool and carried it back to the chemistry lab. After the door shut behind him, I left my hiding spot and raced closer. I felt a rock in my gut when I looked up to see one of the tiny cameras six feet up. That's what Andrew had been adjusting.

My friends were right. It had been Andrew all along.

16

The Exothermic Eruption

THE ROCK IN MY STOMACH MUST'VE BEEN COAL, because now it burned with rage. I couldn't believe I'd actually stood up for that guy. I wanted to rip down the camera and make off with the memory card. I'd take it straight to Mr. Davenport, if he was still in his office. If not, I'd take it home and upload a video of my own. Better yet, I'd give it to Sam to post on her blog. Then everyone could see video of Andrew setting up the camera and the mystery of the blurred blogger would be solved once and for all.

Unfortunately, I couldn't reach the camera. Andrew

was a little taller than me, and he'd needed a stool to get to it. I gave the camera another glance before I turned my attention to the chemistry lab, pulled out my phone, and began recording. If I couldn't use Andrew's video as evidence, I'd get the next best thing—a video of Andrew setting up his next prank.

I marched toward the door, flung it open, and stepped through, my phone at the ready. I spotted Andrew immediately. He sat at one of the worktables, tapping away on his laptop. The lights were off in the classroom, so the glow from the screen illuminated his face.

"There he is!" I said loudly for the camera. "The blurred blogger, minus the blur, setting up his next prank."

Andrew jumped when I entered, but then shook his head. "What are you doing here, Junior?"

"Catching you in the act," I replied, stepping toward him, my phone held out in front of me.

Andrew rolled his eyes. "Why don't you put that thing down and look at this before all your yelling gets everyone's attention?" He pointed to his computer screen.

Honestly, I was surprised how casual he was acting, especially after being caught red-handed. I lowered my phone and glanced at his computer screen. But when I saw the video frozen there, I raised my phone again, needing to capture video of my own.

"I just saw that," I said. "I was down the hall when you were adjusting the camera."

"This is the end of the video, doofus," Andrew said. "I'm not adjusting the camera here. This is me pulling the memory card *out* of the camera." He restarted the video from the beginning. "This is what I want to show you."

The screen showed a jumble of images, like the camera was recording but being jostled. Then the image cleared, and I could see the school corridor outside. The camera seemed to rise off the ground. It was as if I were watching the view from a tiny plane, flying up the side of the wall. The image blurred as the camera rotated 180 degrees. Then I saw a close-up of the culprit in the act of mounting the camera to the wall.

Mr. Osborne.

"No way," I muttered, lowering my phone. I mean, I had guessed it was him, but seeing proof was still shocking.

In the video, our teacher looked over his shoulder, aiming the camera toward the chemistry lab door.

137

When he was satisfied, he climbed down from his ladder, picked it up, and carried it back into the lab. A moment later, he exited with a large white bucket.

"I guessed it was him after I saw the last video," Andrew explained. "You know that 'All right, gang' thing he always says? Super annoying."

"That's exactly what the blogger said," I finished.

"Right." Andrew nodded. "I got the idea when I heard Osborne's voice go deep that day."

"Me too. I told my friends the exact same thing, but they didn't buy it."

"Yeah, right," Andrew scoffed. "Then what was all this . . . 'I caught you in the act' stuff?"

My eyes went wide. "What was I supposed to think? I saw you messing with that camera. I thought I'd been wrong and you were setting up the next prank."

Andrew pointed to the front of the room. "Looks like the next prank is good to go."

In rushing to catch Andrew on camera, I hadn't noticed the huge plastic trash can in front of Mr. Osborne's desk. A tall stepladder (probably the one from the video) stood next to it. I moved closer and turned on my phone's flashlight app, aiming the beam inside the container, and saw that it was about three-quarters full of some strange blue liquid.

"What is this stuff?" I asked.

Andrew shrugged. "Beats me."

I turned off my phone's light and spun back around. "We have to report this."

"You're right about that." Then Andrew nodded toward the wall. "As soon as I grab the cards from the rest of the cameras. I need as much proof as possible to clear my name."

"I can help with that," I offered.

Andrew laughed. "Oh, sure. Because you and your friends have been *so* helpful so far."

"Well, what did you expect after what you pulled at camp? And with Sam? And then you show up here, right when the first prank happens."

"Hey, I didn't plan that." He edged closer. "It's not my fault one of your teachers goes rogue on my first day at this stupid school."

I threw my hands in the air. "Yeah, so, why are you even here, anyway?"

His lips screwed into a grimace. "That's for me to know—"

"Don't give me that. Why don't you tell me the truth for once? Since you were the big man at Bradley, why did you end up here?"

Andrew's eyes flashed with fury. "Because my dad couldn't afford to bail me out anymore, okay? Are you happy now?" He glared at me a moment longer before his shoulders slumped. "Man, I'm here on a scholarship."

"What's wrong with that?" I asked. "Lots of students are. It means that you're here on your own merit. That no one bought your way in." I let out a long breath. "Look, why do you think I work so hard *not* to get special treatment? I want people to know I'm here because I deserve it, not just because my name's on the sign out front."

Andrew cracked a smile. "Yeah, I still don't get that."

I rolled my eyes and laughed.

Andrew shushed me.

"What are you—"

He motioned for me to be quiet again, then pointed toward the door. Someone was whistling as they walked down the hallway. Andrew and I both froze. Maybe the person was just passing by. When the whistling grew even louder, Andrew closed his laptop and ducked behind the worktable. I followed his lead.

The footsteps approached until we heard the door open. Luckily, the worktables were built on top of cabinets, so there was just enough room to conceal both of us from being seen by whoever had entered.

I couldn't help it. I had to take a peek. I guess Andrew felt the same way, since we both leaned out to glance around the table's base.

Mr. Osborne.

The teacher held the same white bucket from the video, except this time it appeared to be full. He grunted as he mounted the ladder, light steam escaping the opening as he climbed higher and higher. If the container was full of hot water, maybe he had gone to the cafeteria to fill it. After all, there was no way that big bucket would fit under the spigots of the smaller sinks in each worktable.

Mr. Osborne groaned as he lifted the bucket over the top of the ladder and set it on the small shelf on the side opposite the rungs. He must've modified the ladder in some way, because after he twisted the bucket, it clicked into place.

He started whistling again as he descended, then moved to his desk and opened a large cardboard box, reached in, and pulled out a tangle of strange objects. He dislodged one from the others—a flat pad, about a third of a square meter, with a long, trailing wire. Flopping the square onto the floor in front of the trash can, he connected the other end of the wire to a small plastic box at the top of the ladder. He did the same thing six more times, until all the squares were laid on the floor.

I was tempted to burst out of hiding and tell him he was busted, teacher or not, but, honestly, I was too busy trying to figure out what he was up to. The strange contraption didn't make any sense to me.

Whatever he was doing, it looked like he'd completed his task. He continued his tune as he grabbed a briefcase from his desk and headed toward the door. I noticed that he was careful not to step on any of the pads as he walked out of the room, closing the door behind him.

Andrew and I waited behind the table until Mr. Osborne's footsteps and whistling faded into nothingness before we slowly stood and edged toward the ladder.

"What was he doing?" Andrew asked.

I moved closer to the ladder. "I don't know."

Steam still wisped from the top of the bucket. I

was about to climb the rungs and look inside when it dawned on me what the pads on the ground were. I put an arm out to stop Andrew from coming any closer.

"What?" he asked.

"Those pads are pressure switches. You know, like the kind you see in haunted houses." I've repurposed some myself from old Halloween decorations, incorporating a few into my own inventions.

Andrew stopped in his tracks. "So, we step on one of those . . ." His eyes followed the wires up to the bucket. "And whatever is in there dumps into the trash can."

Now that I was closer, I could just make out the hinge on the stepladder's shelf. The small black box must operate a quick release of some kind.

Keeping my feet planted where they were, I brought up my phone and shot off a group text to my friends. **Meet me in the chem lab.**

Andrew turned to me and smiled. "Now we've got him for sure." He held up his laptop. "We take this to Davenport, show him the video, and then bring him back to see the latest prank setup." He gestured to the other cameras on the wall. "He can pull those memory cards himself and I'll be totally off the hook."

I nodded. "You're right."

The door flew open as Sam and Amy raced in. Sam grinned when she spotted Andrew next to me. "Caught him in the act, huh?"

I froze. They were about to step on one of the pads.

"Don't move!" Andrew and I cried in unison.

I pointed to the floor. "Those pressure switches will set off the prank."

Sam and Amy froze, their attention on the multiple squares laid out across the floor. Sam looked up at Andrew and her eyes narrowed. "What did you do?"

He laughed. "*I* didn't do anything. It was Mr. Osborne. He's the blurred blogger."

Sam put her hands on her hips. "Oh, really?"

"It's true," I confirmed. "We saw him set up the whole thing."

Amy let out a long breath. "Wow, it's just like you said, Tom."

I motioned to her, then looked at Andrew. "See, I told you I figured it out too."

Andrew waved me off. "Whatevs. At least I can prove that I didn't do it." He carefully stepped toward the door. "I'm going to see if Davenport is still here."

Sam jutted a thumb at Andrew. "He really isn't the prankster?"

"No," I replied. "Andrew has a memory card from one of the cameras. It shows Osborne setting this whole rig up, just like Noah said."

"What did I say?" Noah asked as he stepped into the room. Then he saw Andrew standing beside him. "Oh, hey! You caught him."

"Don't move!" the four of us shouted.

"What?!" Noah almost stumbled out of the room from the verbal assault.

Andrew repeated what we had told Sam and Amy, explaining about the pressure switches and how Osborne was the culprit.

"No way," Noah said. He carefully made his way through the pad minefield and examined the trash can/ladder setup. "What is this one supposed to do?"

"I don't know," I replied as I joined him.

Sam and Amy stepped carefully around the pads to get a better look.

"Some kind of chemical reaction?" Amy suggested.

"Definitely," I said, nodding. "Mr. Osborne has access to all kinds of stuff, remember?"

"Hello, Andy," said an electronic voice behind us. I turned to see that Raider had cornered Andrew in the doorway.

"Ugh," Andrew groaned. "It's Andrew, you stupid robot."

Raider didn't make the correction. Instead, he turned toward us and rolled forward. "Hello, Tom."

My eyes went wide. "Raider, stop!" I ordered.

Noah must've had the same urgent thought. "Stop, stop, stop!" he shouted.

"Hello, Noah," Raider chirped as he rolled forward. "Hello, Sam. Hello, Amy."

In the next instant, the robot rolled over one of the pressure pads and I heard a loud click behind me. I turned just in time to see the shelf drop and the bucket dump clear liquid into the trash can. The reaction was immediate. Blue foam exploded from the can like a volcano.

We tried to get away, but the four of us had been so crowded around the device that there was really nowhere to go, and we fumbled over each other trying to escape. Add to that the fact that we had a large robot at our feet and we didn't stand a chance.

My friends and I yelled as the thick warm foam washed us away like a tidal wave, carrying us toward the door. The last thing I saw was Andrew's terrified expression as he ducked into the hallway. After that, I saw only blue as we were swept into the corridor.

The final prank had been on us.

17

The Absolution Solution

RED-AND-BLUE LIGHTS FLASHED OVER OUR faces from the police car out front as we sat in the academy entryway. The four of us were dressed in matching gym shorts and Swift Academy Fencing team T-shirts. Our other clothes had been stained bright blue and were sopping wet. Andrew, who managed to get away from the prank unscathed, still wore his original jeans and T-shirt. He sat in a chair on the other side of the hallway.

All five of us had been questioned by the police, Mr. Davenport, and even my dad. Andrew had turned over the memory card showing Mr. Osborne setting up the prank, and the police had confiscated the rest of the cameras. One thing was certain: None of us would be stars in the latest blurred blogger video. Of course, after the fact, we all agreed it would've been kind of cool to see footage of us being washed out of the classroom in a tidal wave of blue foam.

Also after the fact, we realized that the last prank actually had a name—elephant's toothpaste. Yeah, that's a real thing. It's a special science experiment, and you can find tons of video demonstrations online. Mrs. Gaines even showed it to us last year. You mix some dish soap, hydrogen peroxide, and a little food coloring. Then you add a water/yeast mixture. The yeast is a catalyst, causing an exothermic reaction. Of course, Mrs. Gaines didn't fill a whole trash can with hydrogen peroxide, so her demonstration hadn't had quite the kick of Mr. Osborne's.

It turned out that Mr. Osborne was still in the building when everything went down. It's really weird watching the cops put one of your teachers in the back of a squad car.

Once the questioning was finished and the police

had driven away, we were all allowed to text our parents to come pick us up. Of course, my ride was already there.

"I have some of my people coming over to clean up the second floor," my dad told us. "Between the mess and the lack of a teacher, I doubt you'll have chemistry class tomorrow."

"Why did he do it?" Sam asked.

My father sighed. "To get back at me for firing him. I think he thought that if he could make Swift Academy look bad, it would make Swift Enterprises look bad by association."

"Whoa," Noah said. "Talk about holding a grudge."

"That's a shame," Amy added. "Mr. Osborne was a good teacher."

"And crazy smart," my father added. "I honestly thought he'd be a better fit over here. But . . . some people take advantage of second chances and some people don't." My dad caught my eye, then glanced over meaningfully at Andrew. "I told Andrew's father I'd give him a ride home."

Boy. Subtle hint there, Dad.

After Amy, Sam, and Noah had been picked up, Andrew and I were alone. My father was still organizing the cleanup detail, so I knew we had some time to kill. *Might as well get it over with.* I got up to join Andrew.

Before I even made it across the hall, he was laughing at me. "Nice outfit, Junior."

I sighed and slumped my shoulders. This kid was really making the whole second-chance thing super difficult.

I plopped down in the seat next to him. "Man, why do you have to be like that?"

He smirked. "Like what?"

"You know . . . mean. Ever since we were kids, you're always putting everything down. Always putting me down. You know I hate when you call me Junior, and you keep doing it. Why?"

"That's for me to know—"

He stopped short as I shot him a look that would've made Sam proud.

"Come on," I said. "We're the only ones here. What's the deal?"

Andrew was quiet for several moments. "Do you remember when we were little? We were best friends, right?"

"Yeah, I do remember." I motioned between us. "That's why I don't understand any of this."

"Well . . ." He let out a long breath. "That was before you thought you were better than me. You got more attention because you were smarter, came up with cooler ideas. I guess I just got sick of it, that's all." He threw up his hands in frustration. "There. Are you happy? Is that what you want to hear?"

I shook my head. "No. Not really. I don't think I'm better than you, and who says I'm smarter?" I pointed at him. "You figured out it was Mr. Osborne, just like I did. You picked up on all the same clues." I glanced around before continuing, lowering my voice. "In fact, we are the only two people in the whole school who figured it out. And this place is crammed full of smart kids."

"Hey." He raised an eyebrow. "I guess you're right."

As we sat in silence, I remembered back to when we were best friends. Sure, we had our disagreements, but we also had our own share of fun adventures back then.

I nudged him. "You remember that time when the wind carried our model rocket into the woods behind my house?"

Andrew grinned and nodded. "Yeah. And it got stuck up in that tree. And then *you* got stuck after you climbed up to get it."

"*We* got stuck," I corrected. "You were right up there with me."

Andrew shrugged. "I was just there to keep you company. I wasn't scared to climb down like you were."

"Yeah, right." I shook my head. "I guess you just kept me company for two hours until our dads found us."

Andrew chuckled. "Well . . . it was a really big tree."

We both laughed as my dad came around the corner.

"All right, fellas," he said, digging his car keys out of his pocket. "You ready to put a period behind another grand Swift Academy adventure?"

"Oh yeah," I replied.

As Andrew and I got to our feet, he let out a snort. "What? Stuff like this happens here a lot?"

I shook my head. "No, not really." Then I shrugged, thinking better of it. "Well, yeah. Kinda. Have lunch with Noah, Amy, Sam, and me tomorrow, and we'll tell you all about it."

Andrew nodded. "All right . . . Tom."